I HATED YOU FIRST

SWORN TO LOATHE YOU - BOOK 1

RACHEL JOHN

Copyright © 2021 Rachel John
Cover Design by Gigi Blume
Cover Illustration by 2sqrdArt

All rights reserved.

No part of this work may be resold, copied, or reproduced without written permission from the author, except for brief quotations used in reviews or articles.

ISBN: 9798515951429

ACKNOWLEDGMENTS

This book is dedicated to my husband's old Chevy truck with the peeling paint. I miss you.

CHAPTER 1

CLAY

How does a twenty-five-year-old mechanic end up dressed as Prince Charming in front of a dozen small children at a backyard party? As you could probably guess, because of a girl. *The* girl. And even though she was completely off limits and hated my guts, there I was, standing in stretchy pants and a floppy hat sporting an ostrich feather. It was complicated. Or very simple, depending on how you want to look at it.

Here's the thing. My best friend, Parker Harwood, has held this enormous grudge against his half-sister for as long as I can remember—some justified, a lot irrational, and all of it highly inconvenient in a family business atmosphere. Also inconvenient? Me carrying a torch the size of a forest fire for her.

If either of them found out, I'd for sure lose them both. And I couldn't lose them. Their messed-up family was all I had.

Having been raised by my grandparents, who left me to my own devices as long as I did my chores, I'd spent most of my childhood at the Harwoods'. I needed them in my life, and that meant keeping my feelings for Lauren to myself.

"Clay, you look like you're constipated," Lauren whispered

out the side of her mouth, waving her gloved hand at all the little birthday attendees sitting on the grass in front of us. "Get ready. The song's coming on."

I got into position on our makeshift dance floor, which was stacks of wooden pallets strapped together, painted a gaudy gold, and bedazzled to death. The Harwoods never did anything halfway, not even the ones who'd married in. I'd be having words with Lauren's sister-in-law later. This was definitely not up to code.

I also didn't appreciate all the cell phone cameras aimed in my direction. There was so much evidence I'd done this.

Facing Lauren, I pressed my palms against her gloved ones. "I hate you so much right now."

That only made her smile bigger. Even dolled up, looking blonde and beautiful and way too princess-like, she couldn't hide her sass. "I know. Thanks for stepping in last minute. This is seriously the highlight of my week."

"Then your week blows." The music swelled, giving me the last word, as I'd hoped it would. I bobbed away from her to the beat, and she did the same on her side. We'd practiced this a couple of times before the party started, and I must have passed some coordination test because Lauren hadn't made fun of me as much as I thought she would.

The wide-eyed kids watching us were awfully cute, I had to admit, but I couldn't wait to change back into my regular clothes and plot how best to cash in this favor. And I *would* cash it in.

Lauren caught the tips of my fingers and rolled into my arms as the song came to an end. I looked down into her big brown eyes and told myself I felt nothing. As usual, it was a lie.

We stepped apart, keeping our fingers linked, and I bowed while she curtseyed. She dropped my hand the second the song ended and jumped down from our pallet kingdom to greet the guests, including the newly five-year-old birthday girl, Raelyn.

I smiled when Raelyn darted around Lauren's poufy dress and came straight for me. I was the fun uncle, even if only an honorary one, and she knew I always carried bubble gum on me.

I unwrapped a piece for Raelyn, and instantly ten other chubby hands came out to beg for one as well.

Lauren pushed her way through them and blocked me, tossing back a glare in my direction. "You can't give gum to the little ones. They'll choke."

A chorus of whining started up, and she shooed them off. "Go get cake in the house. Cinderella's orders."

"Wow, Cinderella is a lot bossier than I remember."

Lauren crossed her arms and turned to face me. "Cinderella is about to be off-duty. Don't forget to give your costume back to Melissa. She has to get it to the costume shop by five or they'll charge her extra."

"What are you in such a hurry for? Hot date?" Not that I didn't know the answer to that. It was Saturday afternoon. Lauren probably had plans with her next flavor of the month. Last I checked, she wasn't dating anyone, but that wouldn't last long.

She gave me a coy smile. "All you need to know is I won't be sitting around refurbishing broken-down air compressors and complaining about the government with you and the boys tonight. Rain check?"

I clutched my chest, pretending her insult hurt. Yeah, I might be a pathetic social exile who hung out with my coworkers on the weekends, but I chose it freely. Every time I asked a girl out, I ended up sorry, whether it was the second our date started or three months down the road when I felt like a trapped hypocrite. My heart wasn't free to give. It already belonged to this spitfire who didn't want it.

I watched Lauren bunch up her shiny blue dress in her fists and take off in a jog towards the house. Her blonde hair in its Cinderella up-do bounced until it came undone and streamed behind her.

CHAPTER 2

LAUREN

Seeing Clay Olsen in a Prince Charming costume today had messed with my head. He was handsome enough already with his mischievous smile and movie-star dimples. It didn't help that he was also strong and tall, and had a smoldering stare he sometimes turned on me when he wasn't teasing me to death. It was all I could do on a normal day at work to make sure he thought I was immune to his charms. Thinking about him on the weekends too was just asking for trouble.

Clay was a jerk, and jerks didn't need to know you found them attractive. It just gave them ammunition to use against you. I didn't know why I was even dwelling on the prince thing anyway.

It was a costume, and not even a good one. He'd looked ridiculous with those tight pants tucked into his boots, his dark, too-cool hair covered up with a velvet hat sporting a jaunty feather, but he'd also filled out that billowing white shirt nicely with the sash going across his chest… Okay, I really needed to think about something else instead of making a pros and cons list of whether or not Clay could light my fire by playing dress up.

It was time to think about my date, who would be here any minute. I took one last look in the mirror before checking my small cross-body bag to make sure I had the essentials. Mints, small hair brush, extra cash, my phone, pepper spray.

Having been raised by an overprotective dad, I wasn't allowed to go anywhere without that last item.

Jenny, my roommate, came into the bathroom and leaned against the door, tucking a wayward lock of her straight red hair behind one ear. "I saw Denver pull up in his Jeep. He's doing a last-minute hair and makeup check, just like you."

"Ha, ha."

Denver did care about his appearance a lot, there was no denying it. But I already got enough ribbing from the guys at work about my choices in men without my roommate piling on, too. Instead of taking the bait and defending Denver, I turned and crossed my arms, ready to use whatever diversionary tactics were necessary.

"What happened to your guy?"

"What guy?" Jenny slipped around me to the bathroom counter and examined my various makeup jars. I'd taken to buying eyeshadow in every color from my favorite Etsy seller. Jenny was less adventurous about makeup—and everything else—but, that didn't mean she didn't like to browse my collection.

"Carpool guy?" I reminded her. "I thought he asked you out."

Jenny wrinkled her cute little nose. Everything about her was little. If I didn't love her so much, I'd banish her to a place where I didn't feel gigantic in comparison with my big feet and long arms.

"He changed his mind."

"He changed his mind?" I'd only asked about him to take the heat off me, but now I was outraged on her behalf. "What do you mean he changed his mind?"

Jenny shrugged. For some reason, it was important for her to act like it wasn't a big deal. "He said with us working together and driving to work together, it was probably a good idea to just be friends. I hate that he's right."

I nodded, although it didn't sound right to me at all. It sounded like an excuse, and nobody should have to experience that sort of backpedaling from the person they cared about. Sometimes dating was the worst.

The doorbell rang and I came out of the bathroom, nudged my feet into the leopard-print flats by the door, and rolled my shoulders back before answering. One nice thing about Denver—he sure knew how to make a girl feel beautiful. I waited while he did that slow smile thing, his signature move of looking me up and down before meeting my eyes, his gaze full of approval.

"You ready to go?" he asked. His skinny jeans were especially skinny tonight, and sort of shiny, as if they were dying to sparkle like a *Twilight* vampire when the light hit them. I could only imagine the jokes I'd get from Jenny about them later.

"Yep." I looked back, and sure enough, Jenny raised her eyebrows at me while running her hands over her thighs. Whatever.

"Have fun, you two." She waved her Sudoku book at us and sank into the couch, pulling down the reading glasses that were almost always atop her head.

I followed Denver out, trying to set aside my worry about Jenny hanging out by herself once again. I knew she craved alone time more than I did, but even introverts had to have a limit, right?

"Why the frown, sunshine?" Denver nudged me with his elbow. His cologne packed a punch tonight. My nose was tingling already.

"Oh, nothing. Work stuff."

Denver opened the passenger door of his Jeep for me, and I got in, making sure to tuck my long legs inside quickly. That way, when he slammed the door, as he always did, no part of me was in the way.

The side of my foot was still recovering from our first date, not that Denver knew. It was nice that he got my door at all, and I hadn't wanted to make things awkward by admitting sometimes his chivalry was a little too enthusiastic.

"What kind of work stuff?" he asked after getting in. He cracked his knuckles, looking concerned. For some reason, he assumed because I was a fleet manager and worked with a bunch of burly guys around heavy machinery, I was knee deep in sexual harassment.

Constant ribbing, yes. Sexual harassment, no. Not a chance; not with my dad as the boss. Denver didn't understand because he hadn't met my dad yet. And there was a reason for that. I avoided having any of my boyfriends meet him whenever possible. I would be his little girl forever, and our relationship was better when I didn't mess with that illusion.

"I was just thinking about the pile of invoices that will be waiting for me on Monday." I waved it off, since it would have been a terrible topic of conversation even if I had been thinking about work. "No work talk. Tell me about this band we're going to see."

Denver drummed his hands on the steering wheel. "It's my cousin's band. They're really good, and I want to support them at their first real gig. You don't mind do you?"

"Not at all. What kind of music do they play?"

"Country. So we're going to this bar with live dancing and music. It'll be great."

I was fine with country music. And dancing. I'd only wished he'd told me more details in advance. I had a pair of cowgirl boots I never wore, but couldn't bear to get rid of.

Denver started up his Jeep and immediately hit the gas, causing me to lurch in my seat until the seatbelt threw me back. His love for his open-top Jeep was so sacred, I think he forgot other people were riding with him half the time. I'd learned from careful experience to pull my blonde hair back into a loose ponytail, hope for the best, and brush it out when we arrived at our destination.

Luckily, the weather was perfect. We were in the last few

weeks of March, when Phoenix was still nice, and we could pretend the summer wouldn't take over soon and crisp us all. I closed my eyes and enjoyed the wind rushing over my face.

Denver turned on the radio, singing along enthusiastically to a Bruno Mars song. He had a great voice and sang as if he knew it.

"Were you ever in a band?" I asked, opening my eyes.

"Oh, yeah. I was the lead singer of *Your Next Crush*. We even made an album before we all went our separate ways for college. Remind me sometime and I'll dig it out."

Your Next Crush. It was so… Denver. I'd never known anyone as easy-going about how full of himself he was. Denver wasn't the guy I wanted to spend the rest of my life with, but dating him was like breathing. I never had to work for it or give it much thought. It didn't even feel like a new relationship. After knowing him a little over a month, I could pretty much predict whatever he was thinking or about to do. Even his surprises were predictable.

Maybe that made me a control-freak, but this was exactly what my life needed right now. Stability, with fun on my terms.

Denver pulled up to the restaurant, which had twinkle lights and a big rooster statue on the roof. After getting my door, Denver took my hand, swinging it back and forth as we walked up to the entrance. I could hear the band going strong before we touched the door. I don't know that I'd categorize it as good country. Earnest, yes. Loud, yes. In key, not quite. Apparently, Denver's cousin didn't get his fair share of the musical talent in the family.

We found two seats at the bar, but we gave them up within seconds as Denver's favorite song was coming on and he wanted to dance. The guy couldn't sit still to save his life. But he also danced as well as he sang, and I couldn't help smiling and laughing, having a great time in spite of the terrible music.

Someone tapped me on the shoulder and I turned, expecting to have to tell some random guy I was taken.

"Evan. Hi!"

My coworker was all cleaned up, with a well-fitting pair of Wranglers and a button down shirt that, for once, wasn't covered in engine grease.

"Hey," he shouted over the music. "You stalking me?"

"Yep, Evan. I just can't get enough of you Monday through Friday."

He laughed and pulled his date over so he could introduce her and I could introduce Denver. There was nothing at all wrong with the situation, except Evan would tell everyone at work I was dating someone new.

And Clay would know.

CHAPTER 3

CLAY

Sun Valley Heavy Equipment Rental was as much a second home to me as the Harwoods' house. Thanks to Parker and his dad's freaky ability to fix just about anything, we'd made a name for ourselves not only as a rental shop, but as the place to sell off finicky equipment. Our side business of buying, trading, and selling had become more and more important as the competition from the big box stores closed in. Everyone was in the equipment rental business these days.

I don't think there was a moment our boss, John Harwood, ever stopped worrying. It wouldn't matter if we had a billion-dollar nest egg. The sky could fall tomorrow and it would all be gone. Day after day, he carried around the responsibility of thirty people who relied on him for their livelihoods. Oh, the joys of owning a small business.

I was inspecting a scissor lift we'd just acquired when Lauren walked in and headed to her desk in the corner to wake up her computer. My Lauren radar always seemed to sense the moment she arrived, and today was no different. Her Sun Valley polo shirt was navy blue today and she was wearing my favorite of her jeans, the ones that had lace on the back pockets.

Idiot brain. It was a good thing no one could read my mind, especially her dad.

If John had his way, his daughter's desk wouldn't be anywhere near the warehouse. She'd be in the front office greeting customers and manning the phone. But Lauren wouldn't stand for it. She was as familiar with the equipment as any of us, maybe more so, because it was her job to track all of it.

Parker came to stand next to me, giving one of the back tires a nudge. "What do you think?" He ran his hands through his dark blond hair, which was several weeks past needing a haircut.

"I'll know more after we change the batteries." Luckily, the scissor lift took the same kind of six-volt batteries as any typical golf cart, including the two we kept on site.

"We bought it without good batteries in it? Without trying it out?" Lauren came over to have a look. "The hydraulics could be all messed up. It could fall over and kill us all." She was slightly taller than Parker, which I knew secretly ticked him off, especially when she leaned over him during an argument like the one they were about to start.

"Good morning to you, too, Lauren." Parker turned to his sister and puffed out his chest. He'd been the one to buy the lift, and his body language showed it was a decision he'd defend with his last breath.

He patted the machine like an old friend. "Everybody wants these, working or not. It was in a storage unit, and they were doing me a favor by calling me first."

"Doing you a favor." She laughed. "More like, they know any time they have a piece of incredibly heavy junk on their hands, you'll be happy to haul it off, and pay them to boot. How much was it?"

"I don't have to tell you. You're not my boss."

"Oh, that's mature."

I stepped between them, knowing things would only get less mature from there if I didn't put a stop to it. I'd been playing the role of peacemaker since we were kids, and while they were a lot more respectful to each other now, it didn't stop these constant work battles. "Let me finish my inspection. Then you can yell at each other with better ammunition."

Lauren sighed. "Okay, sorry. But I'm talking to John about this when he gets back."

"Never doubted that for a minute," Parker called over his back. He was retreating to his workstation, but didn't look happy about it. John would likely side with Lauren on this one, which never helped their sibling rivalry. Parker and Lauren both called him John and not Dad in the shop, but family issues were family issues, no matter the setting.

Now that Parker had backed away, Lauren and I were left standing close together for no particular reason. Her arm brushed mine, leaving a trail of warmth. Moments like this were happening too often. For a long time I'd convinced myself it was totally one-sided, that it was wishful thinking on my part to ever assume she did it on purpose. But my gut said she felt something too, a magnetic connection between us that would only lead to trouble.

Not acknowledging it, letting it be this delicious mystery between us, was not good. And yet, I wasn't about to say something. She'd deny it and make me feel like a jerk. I knew that as well as I knew she'd been wearing those same Converse shoes for three years, and only changed out the laces occasionally.

But if we couldn't talk about it, and couldn't do anything about it, then it was definitely time to make her go away.

"Don't you have more evidence to gather, proving you're better than Parker?"

She slowly shook her head at me. "I don't get you, Clay. Sometimes you're almost nice."

"And that's almost a compliment."

"Hate you," she muttered under her breath.

"I hated you first," I whispered back.

She stalked off, and I went back to changing out the

batteries. These short fixes for our long-term problem were not healthy. I knew it, and yet I didn't know what else to do. It was second nature by now to be the prickly middleman.

The scissor lift performed beautifully, but I didn't put an actual person on it until I'd tried every test I could think of first. Then I made Parker the guinea pig. He was happy to wave at Lauren from twenty feet up in the air.

She ignored him and stared at her computer. He'd won this battle. I would have been happier about it if I thought it would make any difference in their relationship. I sort of understood Parker's inferiority complex. His mom left when he was an infant. Shortly thereafter, Lauren's mom came along and made his dad joyously happy, and then there was a new baby. He was sandwiched in the middle between his over-achieving older brother and the sister he never wanted.

So much of it was in his head. His whole family loved him; well, as much as he'd let them. Lauren had followed us around like an eager puppy when we were kids, hoping Parker would love her half as much as she loved him. She still loved him now, it was just a lot more hidden these days.

He just couldn't appreciate what he had, no matter what they did, and if I picked Lauren over him, it might push him over the edge. I hated that I had to choose at all.

The scissor lift hadn't come with any paperwork, so I jotted down the specs for Lauren.

Evan's cheery whistle echoed through the warehouse, along with the signature jingling of the keys he kept on his belt. "Morning, everyone. Lauren, good to see you again."

Lauren's head shot up, and she pasted on a smile sprinkled with a good helping of anxiety. "Morning, Evan. Don't forget to log your hours on the Komatsu fork lift."

"Will do. Will do." He whistled a tune, something Lauren obviously recognized, based on the way she began fidgeting.

I looked between the two of them, trying to figure out what was going on. Knowing Evan, I wouldn't have to wait long. The guy never shut up.

He set down his coffee cup and rubbed his hands together, looking around. "I saw Lauren at Rooster's Saturday night. She's got a new boy toy," he announced to the group at large.

Herbert smiled before going out for a cigarette break. The man loved gossip, but he loved his nicotine more. John made him smoke on the driveway at the back entrance. Half the time he ate his lunch out there too.

"Congratulations." I approached Lauren's desk and opened up the laptop where we logged repairs.

She could have skewered me with a thousand lasers with the glare she gave me in return. It was a come-hither look as far as my hormones were concerned, but I was used to ignoring those.

She gritted her teeth. "Don't start, Clay."

I held my hands up in surrender. "I'm sure this guy's the one. There's no reason to get all defensive about it."

I couldn't even say it with a straight face. She had every reason to keep her boyfriends a secret from me. I had become an expert over the years in picking them apart, piece by tiny, annoying piece. Not that I could take all the credit. I didn't choose the guys, and I certainly didn't make her break up with them. That was on her. All I did was open up a window of doubt, and she did the rest.

It kept her single, and it kept her hating me. Win-win. Or lose-lose. Sometimes I really despised this game we played.

"Has John met him yet?" I asked.

"Nope." She practically ripped a paper out of the printer and held it out to me half crumpled. "We have someone interested in the Caterpillar 420. They're coming in a half-hour. Make sure it's clean and that Herbert didn't leave any sunflower seed shells in it from when he was working on it, and make sure the hours match what's on here, and take the keys up front." She must have realized how bossy she sounded because she put on what sort of could be considered a smile and added, "Please?"

"As you wish." The words were out of my mouth before I could rethink them.

Lauren's face froze for a second, and then she raised an

eyebrow. "Don't try to butter me up, Clay."

I grinned, taking the paper from her. "Wouldn't dream of it."

She reached out and gripped my forearm before I could walk away. "You won't say anything to John, will you?"

"About the boy toy?" I concentrated on keeping my voice even. The last thing I needed was my voice to crack, or worse, get all breathy with excitement over her touching me.

"I know he'll hear about it anyway, but just..." She released my arm, muttering to herself. "It's hopeless. Evan will tell him the second he sees him."

"I won't say anything to your dad." It was all I could promise her. I couldn't get in the middle of every fight in the Harwood household, especially the ones that involved my boss.

She waved me off, and I went to get the equipment ready, putting my focus on the job where it belonged.

Evan was too busy doing maintenance tasks on our truck fleet to say a word to anybody about anything, and I was relieved. Until John came over and hovered while I replaced the worn out track pads on a mini excavator.

John was never one for idle chitchat. Whatever he had to say, he always came out and said it point-blank. But I still almost drilled one of the bolts into my hand when he opened with, "I want you to break up Lauren and this new boyfriend of hers if things start to get serious."

"And why would you think I'm qualified to do that?" I concentrated on keeping my response casual. This felt like a kick in the pants from Karma, one I should have seen coming.

I tightened the last bolt, and John picked up the worn-out pad I'd taken off, turning it over in his hands. "You've always been like a protective older brother to her. It's no secret Lauren listens when you make fun of whoever she's dating. And you and I both know she's too young to date anyone seriously. Not anyone good enough for her, anyway."

Lauren had just turned twenty-three. How was I, at twenty-five, so much more mature and wise? John never asked who I dated or why. When would Lauren be old enough in his eyes to have a serious relationship? When she was thirty? Forty-five? After he wasn't around to see it? John was a helicopter parent, but this was taking it to a whole new level.

"I'm going to have Lauren bring him to lunch Sunday at our house. Make sure you're there, too, so you can meet him."

I considered declining, but John would insist, even if I had an excuse ready, which I didn't. So, I nodded, focused on my work, and reasoned I could untangle myself from this trap later. But even after John left, I couldn't relax. The more I thought about it, the worse I felt.

John was an observer. Somewhere along the line, he'd caught wind of what I did to Lauren's boyfriends, and now he wanted to mold my gift for his own purposes. I felt exposed. My messed-up relationship with Lauren was a private battle I waged in my head and my heart where no one could see it. Or so I'd thought. Now it belonged to my boss. This wouldn't end with her current boy toy. That much I knew.

CHAPTER 4

LAUREN

Pulling out of the lot after work, I was in the mood for some angry rock music. Not quite the garbage Parker listened to, but something that would match the frustration I felt inside. I settled for a girl power rock band I'd listened to in high school long after it would have been considered cool. In fact, the more Parker and Clay made fun of *Shadow Behind the Sun*, the more I had clung to the band's cheesy, angst-filled lyrics. Their songs filled me with nostalgia for a time when life had been less complicated, when straight A's and not getting speeding tickets was enough to make my dad happy.

Dad had lectured me when I talked to him about Parker's scissor lift purchase. He said I was tattling, as if I'd caught Parker using Mom's good sewing scissors to cut poster board. And yes, I'd tattled that time, too.

Dad didn't get it. We were adults now. I was happy about the scissor lift being a good buy. Anything good for the company was good for me. Team player right here, ladies and gentleman. This was about Parker's undying confidence in making gut purchases. Like gambling, there was an ugly side to any lucky streak. I wasn't being petty; I was trying to be proactive. But Dad missed all that, and when I tried to explain, he'd turned the conversation to the new guy in my life. Or tried to. I shut that down like a strict librarian with chatty patrons.

Once again, I considered leaving the company I loved, the one I'd help build up to what it was today. I'd been battling for my place with Parker and my dad for so long that it was hard to tell whose fault it was that we were like this—so stubborn, so in each other's business. Connor was the smart one. My older brother hadn't worked for the company since high school.

I merged onto the freeway, loving the punchy power of my old '92 Chevy Silverado. Dad had offered to get me a new work truck several times, especially after we had to replace the alternator and the transmission and finally give my Chevy a paint job worthy of the Harwood fleet. But there was no better engine than the small block 350 in this thing, and I'd fight anyone who said differently.

By the time I reached my apartment, I was calm. Jenny stood at the stove making dinner. It smelled amazing.

"Best roommate ever," I said, hanging my cross body bag on a hook and coming into the kitchen to have a look at the stir-fry sizzling in a pan.

"How was work, dear?" she joked. She pointed at the wooden spoon next to the rice pot, silently commanding me to stir. I complied.

"Are you looking for gossip or do you actually want to hear about my work?"

"Gossip, of course."

"My dad found out about Denver."

Jenny laughed. "You hide him like he's a shameful secret. Denver is just about the most respectable specimen you could drag home." She ticked off his qualities on her fingers. "He works for a bank, he has good personal hygiene, nothing on him is pierced, and he takes you on real dates."

"*You* make fun of him." I stole a piece of carrot out of the pan and ate it quickly.

"Too much salt?" Jenny asked.

"Nope, perfect."

"I make fun of him because he's a little too perfect, a little too cookie-cutter. You need someone who's going to challenge you once in a while. And, you know, maybe someone with less gel in his hair."

I sighed. Jenny knew me too well; enough that she could see all the reasons I'd picked Denver out in the first place, even if she didn't fully understand the motivation behind it. Denver was nothing like my family, nothing like Clay, and I liked that.

Clay Olsen. It always seemed to come back to him.

Stupid childhood crush. I'd like to crush it until it was a fun little detour in my history that no one had to know about, like the Justin Bieber poster I used to keep on the back of my bedroom door.

Case in point, after talking to Dad about Denver today, my mind had dwelled on the fact that it was Herbert who told Dad about my boyfriend, not Clay. I'd asked Clay not to say anything, and as far as I could tell, he'd kept his promise.

It shouldn't matter. *He* shouldn't matter. Clay had always been there. I should be bored with him by now, despite his dark blue-gray eyes, his wavy brown hair, and his big strong hands that could fix anything. Stupid crush.

"So, what does this mean? Did your dad ask to meet him?"

"Huh?" I pulled myself out of my thoughts and back to the conversation at hand. "No, but that's not good news. Normal dads ask. My dad? He'll probably recruit a spy or go visit Denver while he's working at the bank and pretend he's interested in a home equity line of credit."

Jenny stopped stirring the meat and vegetables and looked at me. "He'd do that?"

"I certainly wouldn't rule it out. Let's discuss this with food in our mouths."

"So lady-like, Lauren."

"So hungry." I grabbed a plate and dished myself up a nice helping of rice and stir-fry. I loved that Jenny cooked. You would think the more you enjoyed food the better you'd be at making it, but I'd proved that theory wrong over and over again. I couldn't even properly make brownies from a mix.

After a few bites, I continued. "He's never liked anyone I've dated. Okay, he liked one guy, and that turned out to be the biggest disaster of all."

"Because your dad got too attached to him?"

"Because he was my dad's best employee, and he immediately quit after we broke up. His name was Boyce." I didn't like to think about Boyce. I still felt bad about him, and not just because of my dad.

"Boyz?" Jenny leaned forward. "Did you call him Boyz, like Boyz II Men?"

I rolled my eyes. "B-O-Y-C-E. Boyce. And don't try to make everything about Boyz II Men. Your obsession with them is weird. You weren't even born when they had their ten seconds of fame."

"It was way more than ten seconds. They set records with their number one hits."

"Anyway..."

Jenny rolled her hand. "Sorry. Continue. When did you date Boyce with a C?"

"When I was twenty. And my dad has never gotten over it. He still brings him up from time to time. It's not like I deliberately tried to ruin his favorite employee."

Jenny swirled rice around her plate. "Dating coworkers is always tricky. I'm assuming you were working there, too, right?"

"I was. But let's change the subject. Anything new at your work?" I asked.

She shrugged. "My boss is one inappropriate comment away from me reporting him to H.R., and Noah, the carpool guy who asked me out is... just my coworker now. Today, we didn't talk the whole ride to work, and once we were at work, we talked about nothing but collating."

"Collating? Like, making copies?"

"Yep. We had a ten minute conversation on the best page order for the booklets and possible staple placements for the binding. Titillating stuff right there."

I smirked. "Well, if he turned a thirty-second conversation into ten minutes just to stand next to you, that's sorta hot. Did he lean over and whisper in your ear?"

"Ew, no. That's the type of thing my boss does, and then he gets all offended and flabbergasted when you call him out on it. Noah kept a respectable distance, hands behind his back and everything."

"He kept his hands behind his back because he was afraid his feelings would show if you two accidentally touched and he dropped all the papers on the floor."

Jenny narrowed her eyes at me, trying not to laugh. "Your interpretation of my day is so much more romantic than my reality. Go on. Tell me more."

I was embarrassed now, but Jenny's know-it-all-smirk had me accepting her challenge. "Well, naturally, you'd have to stoop down and help him pick up all those papers, and then your eyes would meet and then your mouths, and then… then…" I rubbed my palms together. "Someone would walk in and you'd both have to scramble to your feet and pretend you were checking each other's lips for leftover frosting from the birthday cake at lunch."

"What birthday cake?"

"You work with like five hundred people. It's always somebody's birthday, right?"

Jenny grinned. "Pretty much. So, in your fantasy, do we get caught making out or do they buy the whole, 'I-was-cleaning-the-frosting-off-his-lips-for-him' excuse?"

"They're suspicious, but they let it go. After that, the two of you just give each other looks of mournful yearning from across the hall. It's very tragic."

Jenny sighed. "Lauren, the secret romantic."

"Emphasis on secret." I had a tough-girl image to protect, after all.

My phone rang in the other room where I'd left it on the arm of the couch. I ran and grabbed it, assuming it was my mom or sister-in-law. Denver wasn't one to call and check in. In fact, the only thing that would make him call anyone instead of text was if he'd suddenly been turned into Edward Scissor Hands, and even then, he'd probably use voice-to-text.

It was a surprise to see Parker's name. He did call occasionally, but never after a spat at work. We usually just pretended like it never happened; the Harwood version of a truce.

"Hi, Parker."

Jenny lost interest upon hearing it was my brother and got up to refill her glass with ice water. Business calls bored her to tears.

"Hey Lauren, I have great news for you." The sarcasm in Parker's voice didn't fill me with confidence about what was coming next. "There's an Aichi bucket truck for sale in Boise, Idaho, and Dad is insisting I fly with you to check it out and haul it back. I guess you're the expert on Japanese bucket trucks now."

"Idaho. Yay." I did not want to drive home in a bucket truck from Idaho, especially with Parker taking me along as punishment. This was Dad's version of sticking us in the timeout T-shirt together until we stopped fighting. But if he'd found the bucket truck holy grail, we didn't have a choice. Most of the ones we wanted shipped straight from Japan at a price we couldn't afford. Finding a decent used one in the U.S. was worth a lot of driving. "How tall is the lift?"

"Ninety-two feet."

I whistled. Those *were* hard to find. "What year?"

"2005. Look, I can email you all the specs. But what I really want you to do is talk Dad out of making you go. I'm the one who works on these. I know what they're worth, and I know what to look for. You'll just slow me down with bathroom stops. No offense."

"None taken. You should take someone with you, though. Just in case you break down."

"You worry too much. Maybe Clay can come along and babysit me. Would that make you feel better?"

"Yes. But only if you cut the attitude, Parker. It's a little much, even for you."

"Sorry. I just hate having Dad as my boss. It's not even that I want to be the boss instead. It's just..."

"Trust me, I get it. And I'll talk to him tomorrow about not making me go along with you. If I call him now he'll know you asked me to."

"True that. Thanks, Lauren."

I put my phone down and fiddled with the last bite of my dinner. I wasn't sure if the business was what kept our sibling relationship going or what constantly tore it apart. Sometimes it was both. Parker was really cool when he wasn't trying to be such a jerk.

Did Clay treat me the same way out of solidarity, or did I truly annoy him, too? Occasionally, when Parker wasn't around, I'd catch Clay looking at me, really looking—the way a jewel thief might stare at a priceless necklace encased in glass. Or maybe it was just my active imagination. My secret romantic side, as Jenny liked to point out.

"What was that about?" Jenny offered to take my now empty plate along with hers, but it was my turn for dishes, so I took hers instead and brought them to the sink.

"My dad is trying to make me and Parker take a road trip together."

"With Clay along, too?" Jenny smirked. "Do it."

"No way."

She'd been relentless since the day she'd seen the two of us together, which was for literally about thirty seconds three months ago. My truck had been acting up, and Clay picked me up for work since he lives close by.

Jenny didn't buy my promises that the two of us were like brother and sister. I didn't buy it either, but I'd keep trying to convince us both.

I also wouldn't be accepting rides from Clay anymore. He made me listen to sports talk radio and wouldn't turn down the air conditioning in freaking January. Even when I closed the vents on my side of his truck, I froze. An all-day road trip in a bucket truck with him and Parker would be a pleasure I'd gladly help wriggle my way out of.

CHAPTER 5

CLAY

I rolled over and silenced my alarm. The dream I'd been having before being rudely awakened slipped away like sand through my fingers. I was pretty sure Lauren had been in it, based on how badly I wanted to return to the land of the unconscious, but now that I was awake and aware, it was better to let it go.

Thinking of Lauren reminded me of yesterday and her dad's boyfriend-breakup request, and the stress of it returned, especially after I remembered we had a company meeting first thing. I hoped John wouldn't say anything stupid in the meeting today; anything that might upset the status-quo between me and Lauren, as imperfect as it was.

But there was no use laying here speculating. I jumped up and showered, ate, dressed, and gathered up my things. Living alone was new to me. I'd had roommates for years, including Parker, but I'd jumped at the opportunity to buy this townhouse when the market took a dive and the interest rates were crazy low.

Sometimes the quiet got to me, but mostly I loved doing my own thing at my own pace and not having to move around other people and tolerate their odd habits or noises. Parker, for example, used to put his initials on everything with permanent marker. His milk carton, the tags of his shirts, the bottoms of his shoes, even his beloved kitchen appliances, like his Vitamix blender.

Strangely enough, he probably missed having roommates more than me. At least, based on how often he was over here. A pair of his socks with P's written on the toes were still on the living room floor from our movie marathon the other night.

I flipped off the kitchen lights and locked up before jumping in my truck parked outside, only to hear the dreaded click, click, click, telling me I had a dead battery. Perfect. I'd become too reliant on getting to work with mere minutes to spare, and now it was going to bite me in the butt.

Parker, ever punctual, would already be at work. I mapped out other options in my mind, trying to deny the obvious choice, which was to call Lauren and have her swing by. The longer I waited, the less likely she would still be at home.

I sat up straighter as I scrolled to her number, putting my game face on like I was psyching myself up for the high jump in track. Talking would be faster than text, and yeah, I also wanted to hear her surprise at hearing from me because I'm whipped like that.

"Clay?"

"Hi, Lauren. Have you left for work yet?"

"I'm leaving now. Why?"

"My truck decided it was your turn for a favor."

She laughed. "I thought your beautiful new Ford was problem free. It was only my hunk-of-junk Chevy that was allowed to have a bad day."

"All I need is a jump from you. A dead battery is a little different than transmission failure after 300,000 miles."

"Insulting my truck while asking for a favor? Bad form, Clay."

"Okay, I'm sorry. Your truck is beautiful and will live forever. Now will you please come give me a jump?"

"That'll take too long and we'll be late for the company meeting this morning. I need John in a good mood. Just get in my truck as soon as you see me, and after the meeting, I'll come back with you. Or Parker will come back and help you jump it." With that, she hung up.

I should have been irritated knowing I'd have to deal with my truck later, but I smiled and got out, leaning against my truck to wait. The Palo Verde trees in my yard were in full bloom, leaving yellow fluff on everything they touched. Later this summer, they'd drop ugly seed pods everywhere because, why not? If it didn't take so long to grow trees, I'd uproot them and plant something that didn't make such a mess.

Two neighbors drove off while I waited. I could have asked either one of them for a jump, but when it came to inconveniencing people, it was better to stick with those who didn't feel obligated to be polite. I hated asking strangers for favors. Which reminded me I should probably meet my neighbors beyond the occasional head nod.

Speaking of people who didn't feel obligated to be polite, Lauren finally pulled up in her Chevy and lowered the driver window. "Get in, loser."

I rounded the hood and jumped in the passenger seat. "Morning, Harwood."

"Morning, Clayton."

Only my grandparents, and Lauren when she wanted to annoy me, used my full name. She turned her peppy music back up and purposely ignored my reaction to hearing it. Which was a shame. My look of disdain was legendary.

"Is this *Shadow Behind the Sun*?"

"Yes, it is. Thanks for asking. Are you hot?"

"Some girls say I am. Thanks for asking."

She gripped the steering wheel tighter. I'd totally foiled her plans to rub it in that she was sweating me out by withholding air conditioning. It was a little stuffy, but I wouldn't be saying a word no matter how warm it got in here.

She looked me over, probably hoping for another way she could make my life miserable during the short trip to the office.

"Put your seat belt on, Clay."

"Make me."

That was a mistake. As soon as we pulled up to the stop sign on the corner, she threw the truck in park, reached across the bench seat, and pulled my seatbelt across my chest, giving me a nice whiff of her shampoo. The only way I could describe it was sexy bubble bath scent. I didn't resist her seat belt enforcement, afraid a tussle might turn into what I was imagining in my head.

She caught my expression as she pulled away, before I hid my reaction to her invading my space. The look she gave me in return was... contemplative. Not good.

"It's your turn to go," I pointed out. The car behind us agreed by laying on the horn.

Lauren put the truck in drive and stepped on the gas. She and that gas pedal were good friends. I had a feeling she'd charmed her way out of several speeding tickets over the years.

She tossed her blonde hair over one shoulder. "At least by giving you a ride, we're even now for the Prince Charming thing."

"Not a chance. I gave you a ride a few months ago, so we're even as far as rides go. The Prince Charming favor will be coming, as soon as I figure out what I need from you."

"The adoration and thanks of my little niece wasn't enough?"

"Nope." Though I hadn't even remembered the favor Lauren owed me until she mentioned it. It felt like she was egging me on, and that made me a little wary about calling in a favor. Maybe that was her plan. Reverse psychology. There was no way I'd let her get away with that. A favor was a favor, and she'd pay up soon.

"Why do you need John in a good mood?" I asked, changing the subject.

"What?" She turned, looking flustered.

"You said you needed him in a good mood. Why?"

"Oh, I don't know. He wasn't happy that Parker and I got into it over the scissor lift yesterday."

There was more to it than that, but I'd get better information out of Parker.

We pulled up to a stop light and Lauren looked me over again.

"Planning your next attack?" I asked.

"You have something yellow in your hair."

It was probably Palo Verde tree fluff. Before I could lower the mirror and check for it myself, she put the truck in park and reached over, plucking a piece out and lingering close to my face as she brushed her fingers through the rest of my hair, searching for more. Yeah, she knew exactly what she was doing to me.

I swallowed hard. "Your boyfriend doesn't mind it when you fix another guy's hair?"

She immediately retreated, looking insulted. "He's not my boyfriend. We haven't really put a title on what we are yet. And no, he wouldn't mind me pulling yellow fluffy things out of your hair because you're like a brother to me." She shivered. "Gross."

I put my hands up. "I was just trying to be fair to the guy. No need to throw up in your mouth a little."

Her responding grin suddenly turned into a frown. "Ugh, I fell right into your fishing for information trap, didn't I? Are you going to report to John that I don't consider Denver my boyfriend?"

"His name is Denver?"

She smacked my arm before turning her focus completely to the road, and no matter what I said for the remainder of the drive, she remained silent. Mission accomplished. The second we parked, she grabbed her stuff and took off. It was better if it didn't look like we'd arrived together anyway.

CHAPTER 6

LAUREN

There was something seriously wrong with me. I *had* been toying with Clay, and whether or not it would have bothered Denver, it was certainly bothering me that I couldn't seem to help myself. How could flirting and fighting walk such a thin line? Sometimes I just wanted to see how far I could push things to get a reaction out of Clay, like he triggered my competitive nature or something.

He was my co-worker, my enemy, my brother's best friend, and my dad's lackey. I had a million reasons to keep me from ever considering Clay as anything other than a nuisance, so why wasn't I acting like it?

I cleared my thoughts the best I could and squared my shoulders before walking into the conference room, where almost everyone was already seated at the table staring at their phones. My dad turned around from the white board and raised one eyebrow when he saw me. To him, five minutes early was five minutes late, especially when it came to our mandatory safety meetings.

Clay slipped into his seat right as Dad was writing talking points on the board.

Dad would write a follow-up email with the minutes of the

meeting, but I took my own notes. Attitudes were contagious, and when Parker and I paid attention, so did the rest of the guys. With the size of our small company, even one more recordable incident would have OSHA all over our backs.

The guys had gotten lax about wearing their ear and eye protection, not to mention the cigarette butts Dad found near the welding equipment. He gave our three smokers a verbal tongue-lashing that had all of us wincing. Of course, if he didn't threaten to fire us all at least once, it wasn't a Tuesday.

After the meeting, Clay tilted his head towards Parker to let me know they'd take care of getting his truck jumped, and I was relieved.

I went back to my desk and went through the equipment logs, checking to make sure everything had been returned that morning as scheduled. No one bothered me for a blessed hour until Dad loomed over my desk, bearing donuts.

That was never a good sign, but I took a glazed treasure from him anyway.

"What's up, John?"

"Did Parker tell you about the Idaho trip?"

"Yes." I kept my eyes on my paperwork. "Is it worth going all the way to Idaho for? I haven't seen the specs."

"We're in negotiations with the owner now, but yes, it's worth it."

"I don't think Parker needs me along then, do you?" I looked up, trying to appear nonplussed, as if the thought had only just occurred to me.

"I'd really like you two to go together."

"Clay could go. He'd actually get Parker to take turns with driving the thing." I knew from experience Parker would have to be on death's door to let me take the wheel.

"I need Clay here, and it would be good for you and Parker to spend some time together. I trust you'll get the job done no matter who's driving."

Parker was going to hate me if I failed him. I took a bite of donut and tried to think of my next plan of attack.

Dad shrugged. "Of course, maybe I could let you off this one time if you'll promise me one thing."

Crud. He'd led me right into a trap. I'd never been the one ahead in this conversation. "Oh yeah?"

"Your mother is planning a nice family luncheon for this Sunday and we'd love it if you'd bring the young man you're dating."

"Dad, that is so unnecessary. We've only been out on a couple of dates."

"How many is a couple?"

"Like four or five." It was actually more like six or seven, but you couldn't call it a date if you stopped for Burger King, right? "He won't be asking for my hand anytime soon if that's what you're worried about."

"I'm not worried, but you seem to be. I promise we'll be nice. No grilling whatsoever. Except for the steaks."

He smiled at his own joke, and I couldn't help smiling back. "And if I bring him, I don't have to go to Idaho? That's what you're saying?"

"That's what I'm saying."

This was so unfair. But maybe Denver wouldn't be available anyway. I didn't have any control over his schedule. "Fine. Deal."

Dad left me in peace to finish my donut and my work. Unfortunately, peace at work was a fleeting thing. Within minutes, Evan came over and pulled up a chair. He needed to log information on the laptop we kept on the end of my desk, but that never stopped his mouth from running while he did it.

"Hey, Lauren. How's it going?"

"Not great." I closed up the invoice I'd been looking at and crossed my arms. "The next time you see me around town, forget you ever saw me, okay?"

Evan's eyes widened. "Okay."

"I'm not saying don't come say hi to me. I'm saying, don't come in here the next day and report on who I'm dating. It's rude."

"Yes, ma'am. I'm sorry. I didn't mean anything by it, but I can see now why that might bother you." Evan looked down at the keyboard, continuing his hunt and peck method of typing. Somehow, even when he did the stupidest things, it was impossible to stay mad at him. He was just so nice, and he'd gained enough experience in apologizing that he'd gotten really good at it. Evan also had wholesome, boy-next-door looks that let him get away with more than he should. Luckily, he was too sweet to know he could use it for evil.

Evan looked up from his typing again. "Clay's truck didn't start this morning. He and Parker went to go get him a new battery."

"I know." I didn't want to admit to giving Clay a ride, but if Evan found out, he might wonder why I'd tried to hide it. "He rode with me this morning."

"Oh yeah?" Evan smiled. "I think it's so cool the three of you got to grow up together. My family moved all over the place."

I'd heard Evan talk about moving a lot when he was growing up, but never with the wistful tone he had now. It made me feel guilty for fighting so much with Parker and resenting Clay's very existence. Well, a little bit guilty. They were stinkers, and we would be eternally locked in a battle where I had to fight for my place in their stupid loyal friendship. I wasn't naïve enough to think Parker would be nicer to me if he didn't have Clay, but sometimes it seemed like Clay fit in better with my family than I did.

Evan scratched his head. "Yeah. The last time we moved was a week before Prom. And being a dumb teenager, I asked a girl, hoping the move wouldn't work out."

"Oh, no."

"Yeah, she didn't take it well." He was quiet after that for several minutes, which might possibly have been a record. I pulled up the next invoice due for payment.

"Do you think my scruff is annoying?" he asked, scratching his chin. At some point or another, the guys were always trying out facial hair, and Evan must have decided it was his turn. He looked like he was two weeks out from a good shave.

"Well, it's obviously annoying you. Quit scratching it like that."

"But do you think it looks annoying?"

"Yes. I think you should shave." He'd asked, so I decided to be honest. It was growing in uneven, and would only look worse with time.

"Good to know. My girlfriend won't ever tell me if she doesn't like something, but I knew you'd give it to me straight."

I laughed. "I'm mean like that."

He tried to backpedal and only made it worse, which was so typical Evan. I got another of his splendid apologies, followed by a story about how his dog learned to open the refrigerator by pulling on both sides of the kitchen towel on the door. Evan was great at distracting people. Not something to put on a resume, but helpful today, when there were so many things I didn't want to think about.

It wasn't until the drive home, when I realized I now had to actually invite Denver to my family's luncheon, that I felt like hitting something again. I waited to text him until I was home, with my shoes off, and I'd watered my house plants. I typed out a message while scanning the fridge for dinner options.

Lauren: Hey, want to be my plus-one at a family luncheon this Sunday?

Denver: Cool. Cool. This sounds fancy tho. What do I wear?

Lauren: Preferably clothes. It's a BBQ.

Denver: Clothes optional. 10-4.

"What a dork," Jenny said, from right over my shoulder.

I jumped, and my phone jumped out of my hands before I reclaimed my grip on it. "Jen, don't sneak up on me like that!"

"I was standing right here. You had phone blindness."

I *had* been concentrating awfully hard, debating whether to warn Denver that my family could be intense or just let it be a surprise. Maybe, as good natured as Denver was, he wouldn't notice.

"What's this about a clothes-optional barbeque?" Jenny reached around me and grabbed a yogurt.

"I was inviting Denver to my family's thing on Sunday."

Jenny put her hands on her hips. "I thought you didn't want your dad to meet him."

"I don't." I took out the milk and put it on the table before getting a bowl and spoon. Cereal for dinner, baby. "I got tricked into it."

Jenny sat across from me and tucked her knees up, wrapping her arms around them. "This ought to be good."

I relayed my dad's evil plan to make me choose between two things I didn't want to do. The more I thought about it, the more diabolical it seemed. My dad had clearly missed his true calling as a CIA interrogator.

Jenny reached over and took a handful of Honey Nut Cheerios out of the box next to me. "Who comes to these Sunday lunches? I mean, besides your brothers and your sister-in-law and the kids? Is that it?"

"Maybe the O'Dells. They've lived across the street from us since I was in diapers, and they love free food and family drama. We provide large helpings of both. And Clay sometimes..." Shoot. Clay might be there. Since I'd never brought a guy home, that had never bothered me before, but there was no way I'd bring Denver over if Clay was there to observe us like specimens in a jar.

I looked up to see Jenny watching me, eating another handful of Honey Nut Cheerios like it was buttered popcorn and I was her favorite movie. "Clay and Denver *and* your family. Have fun with that."

"Not Clay. I'll make sure he's not there." If luck was on my side, I wouldn't have to say anything, and he wouldn't show up. But luck was rarely on my side, especially when it came to Clay. Considering he had responded with "make me" after I asked him to wear a seatbelt, I wasn't getting my hopes up.

CHAPTER 7

CLAY

Parker and I hadn't been on a road trip together in years, and it felt like we were slipping back into old times, except that I spent most of the time working on my laptop rather than trying to beat my record in Angry Birds. John only let me come on the condition that I take an online certification class while we drove home. It was one of those classes that wouldn't let you continue to the next page until their clock said you'd spent enough time on the quiz at the bottom. I don't think I could have physically sat through all ten hours of this class anywhere else but in the cab of a bucket truck.

"Thirty miles to Las Vegas. We might be home by midnight after all." Parker shifted in his seat. "Do you remember the girl in our science lab I was always partnered with? Denise?"

"Junior year?"

"Yeah. I ran into her at the grocery store the other day, and she asked me out. She asked about you, though."

Oh, *that* Denise. I remembered her. She had used Parker's crush on her to try to get close to me in high school. Not cool. "So, are you going out with her?"

Parker scoffed. "No. If you were happily married and living in another state, yes, I'd totally go out with her, because she's still hot. But no. She's also still completely interested in stalking you. I gave her your address and the passcode to turn off your security system."

I lightly punched him in the arm and stole a Starburst from the bag he had perched on the console. "It's too bad you didn't run into the other Denise. The one from college."

Parker frowned. "No, that ship has sailed. I do still like short, angry brunettes though."

"I'll keep my eyes peeled for one."

"Keep an eye out for yourself. When was the last time you dated anybody?"

"Too long." I did not want to have this conversation with him, especially while picturing Lauren, wondering what she was up to right now. She liked us to think she was out having fun all the time, but Lauren was a homebody at heart. She was probably sitting on her couch in front of her TV, balancing dinner on her lap, wearing yoga pants, fuzzy socks, and a tank top. That's what she'd worn to bed in high school. Not that I'd noticed or anything. I focused back on the page of technical jargon and flicked myself in the jaw for good measure.

"You getting tired?" Parker glanced at me. His sharp eyes missed nothing. "I'm good to drive the rest of the trip."

"I'm fine. If you get tired, let me know." I watched the countdown clock until the page let me move on. My phone, which had been sitting in one of the cup holders of the truck's console, lit up with a text message, and when I saw Lauren's name I immediately picked it up.

Lauren: Having fun?

Clay: Just tell me what you're fishing for, Harwood.

There was no way she'd texted me without a motive. The Harwoods were wired for scheming, Lauren included.

Lauren: Play nice. Thanks to me, you're sitting there and I'm not.

Clay: So you're to blame? I'm hour 9 into a 10 hour certification class.

Lauren: Aw, that's so sad. Tell me more.

Clay: Seriously, Harwood. What gives?

Lauren: I was just checking on you guys. I know Parker insisted on driving so I thought I'd text you.

I was smiling too much, and Parker noticed. "Who's that?" he asked, nodding at my phone.

I froze, not sure whether to lie or not. There wasn't anything inherently flirty in our exchange, but the fact that it existed made me hesitant to share it. I finally scrolled up to just show the last bit and read it to him, holding it out so he could see.

Parker shook his head. "She knows me well. Tell her not to worry so much."

Clay: We're fine. We'll be home about midnight.

I went back to my certification and forced myself not to check my phone, though it lit up again.

The second Parker was out of the truck at the next gas station, I picked up my phone and dialed her. She answered on the second ring.

"Hi, Clay."

"Lauren, you have about ten seconds to tell me what's up. Parker's pumping gas, and I do not want to have a conversation with him about why you keep texting me. Mainly because I don't know why you keep texting me."

She was quiet for about nine of those seconds, and then she blurted it all out. "Parker begged me to find a way to not have to go with him on the Idaho trip. And my dad, being my dad, said I was off the hook if I brought Denver to lunch this Sunday."

Wired for scheming. All of them.

Lauren sighed. "Bringing him to my parents' house is going to be hard enough as it is. Promise me you won't be there with your judging eyes and snide comments. All I'm asking is for you to skip this one."

"What if I just promise to leave the judgments at home?"

"Clay Olsen, I will end you right now."

Her bluster had always made me laugh, and even though I felt terrible about it, I couldn't help finding it funny now. "Oh, yeah? You're going to kill me through the phone, darling?"

"No, I'll wait outside your house tonight and jump you when you walk up to your door."

"Don't threaten me with a good time." I could barely get the words out, I was laughing so hard. "And just a heads up, if you're planning a surprise attack, it's best to keep it a surprise. You'll get better results that way."

She growled and hung up on me, not that I could blame her. Making her mad was just too much fun. I jumped out to stretch and go use the bathroom before we hit the road again. This was our last stop before home.

Even with the massive machine we were driving, we made good time. I hadn't decided whether or not I was listening to Lauren's ultimatum or John's about Sunday, but I have to say I was more than a little disappointed Lauren wasn't lurking in the bushes when Parker dropped me off at my house just past midnight.

CHAPTER 8

LAUREN

Denver's humming was not helping me in my attempts to clear my mind and relax. We were driving in my truck to my parents' house for lunch, and he was the coolest cucumber in the fridge. Meanwhile, I was wondering if I could find a way to spill something on myself when we got there so I could borrow one of my mom's shirts. The one I was wearing already had nervous sweat on it. The kind they talk about when they say you can smell fear.

Don't get me wrong; I loved my family. But they were a rough-around-the-edges band of misfits, and they didn't take the idea of adding someone lightly. My sister-in-law included. I'd thwarted her every attempt to set me up with guys in the past, knowing she wouldn't be able to keep herself from getting involved. Which meant there was a good chance she wouldn't like Denver simply because she didn't get to pick him out.

This stunk. I didn't even care if they liked Denver. I just didn't want them to scare him away. Denver was exactly what I needed right now, someone content to just hang out with me on the weekends without trying to take things further than I wanted, physically or emotionally. Where would I find that anywhere else?

"Lauren, you look like you're ready to drive us straight out of town and keep going."

"What?" I turned to look at Denver, who was grinning at his joke, the one I'd apparently missed.

"What's the matter? Are you afraid your family is going to embarrass you? Or not approve of me or something?"

I fiddled with the air conditioning vents, trying to get them to blow inside my sleeves without being super obvious about it.

Echoing Jenny's words, I finally said, "How could anyone not approve of you?"

Denver shrugged. "I am amazing."

"And humble."

"I'm pretty much the perfect package."

I swear he was only half-joking, which made me laugh. "My family is weird. I'll just put that out there, and if they act fine, then I'll retract it and say I'm the one who's weird, and we'll never talk about this again."

Denver shrugged. "It's a meal. What can go wrong at a barbeque?"

"You're so chill about everything. I wish I could bottle it up and sell it."

"I'm so chill, Frosty the Snowman hangs out in my yard just to live longer."

"Dork."

We turned the corner where Clay's grandparents lived in a small white stucco house with a red tile roof. Their yard looked perfectly trimmed, just the way it always had. I wondered if Clay was responsible for it now. He'd worked in that yard every Saturday growing up. I could still picture him making rows with the lawnmower, occasionally lifting his shirt and wiping his forehead. On the really hot days, he'd been shirtless. He'd always tanned well. Aaand cut. Those memories would not be tap dancing through my thoughts anymore today.

I pulled up to the curb behind my brother's minivan. Melissa, my sister-in-law, was attempting to heft Jax's car seat out; no small feat. Jax had rolls for days, the kind grandmothers liked to pinch. I'd be loving up on my favorite six-month-old A.S.A.P.

Little Raelyn ran over to my truck and opened my door.

"How's my Cinderella birthday girl?" I asked.

"Good." She spotted Denver and immediately turned shy.

"Raelyn, this is Denver."

"Okay, bye." She ran off, ignoring her parents' calls for help bringing things in. I got out and Denver followed me over to the minivan, where I took bags of chips and rolls from my brother, and Denver got handed a crockpot.

"Welcome to the family, dude." Connor clapped him on the back, probably meaning to be intimidating. Like me, he'd gotten the height in the family, plus a build that made you think he still worked on cars and not in a dental office. "We'll put you to work first thing here. Do you know anything about motors?"

"Um, I—"

"Connor, knock it off. Be a gentleman and go take your ginormous baby from your wife before her arms fall off."

It was the perfect distraction. Connor ran to catch Melissa and took Jax from her. But that, unfortunately, freed Melissa to take her turn embarrassing me. I could see it in her eyes. She just couldn't help herself, which was why she fit into our family perfectly.

She waited for us to reach her at the porch steps before leaning in and inspecting my left hand. "Where's the ring?"

"Melissa, seriously?"

"What? Too soon?" She winked at Denver. "Lauren swore up and down she wouldn't bring home a man without a ring on her finger. You must be something special because she's as picky as they come. Congrats on meeting her ridiculously high standards."

I waited until she turned to go up the steps before checking for Denver's reaction. My cool cucumber looked a little pickled. "She's joking. They're both joking, Denver. I swear."

He nodded, adjusting his grip on the crockpot. "For sure."

Well, we were off to an excellent start. I couldn't wait to find

Dad, prove I'd brought the victim, and get the heck out of there.

I led the way inside past the living room where my brother and sister-in-law were unlatching Jax and into the large, spacious kitchen my mom had painstakingly remodeled. Cooking was her passion. One thing was certain, the food would be good today.

"Mom!" I'd never been happier to see her in my whole life. She put down the knife she'd been using to spread garlic butter across French bread halves and gave me a squeeze. We shared the same blonde hair, though hers was peppered with a little bit of gray at the roots these days.

"Give him something to do," I whispered. "I'm borrowing a shirt, okay?"

She gave me a strange look, but moved around me to say hello to Denver and immediately assigned him to mix the ranch dip. Moms are the best. I escaped down the hall to my parents' bedroom and straight into their closet where I flipped through my mom's shirts, looking for something similar to the peach-colored T-shirt I was wearing. I finally settled on a pale pink one I knew Mom wouldn't mind me borrowing. It didn't squeeze me in as much as the one I had on, and trading shirts almost felt like a do-over. This was my chance to be calm and collected from here on out. Well, after I had a little talking-to with Connor and Melissa.

I walked back to the kitchen with an Enya song playing in my head. I was totally calm. Frosty the Snowman level of chill. "Where are Dad and Parker?" I asked.

Mom sighed. "Checking on the shop. An alarm went off, and the night watchman doesn't come in until tonight."

It was an annoying but common problem. Hopefully, it was just an oversized pigeon this time and not a thief trying to break in and steal equipment.

"What's your favorite thing to eat, Denver?" Mom asked.

Finally, a normal, non-invasive question. What was wrong with the rest of my family?

Denver started telling her about some amazing side dish

called cowboy caviar, and I seized the opportunity to stalk back to the living room where Connor and Melissa were practically setting up a nursery for Jax. They had a swing, his bouncer, a play mat, and burp cloths everywhere. The kid spit up like a champion, and nothing was sacred, especially furniture.

"Did you change your shirt?" Melissa asked.

"Yes, don't change the subject."

They both gave me a blank look, and I realized the argument I'd started with them in my head hadn't escaped my mouth yet. I was totally losing it.

"What's wrong with you guys?" I hissed. "Denver and I are not engaged—not anywhere near it. So, stop freaking the poor kid out."

"The poor kid?" Connor smirked. "I guess we know who wears the pants in that relationship."

I closed my eyes, trying to think of any leverage I held over Connor. But there was none. He didn't even work with us. Fixing cars was a hobby for him when he wasn't fixing teeth.

"Melissa, if you love me at all, you will throw me a bone here. I'll never see Denver again after today if you two keep this up, and if that happens, there will be no babysitting for you. None." I avoided looking at Jax, who was blowing raspberries, like an audible photobomb to our conversation.

Melissa blinked in surprise. "You must really like him." In retrospect, I should have noticed the way her eyes slid from my face to somewhere behind me, but I was so worked up I didn't care who heard us.

"I just need his type right now, okay?"

"And what type is that?" Denver's arms came around me from behind. I felt like the hugest jerk.

"The type who doesn't judge me based off of my meddling family. That's who." I turned around and hugged him, planting a kiss on him for good measure.

He smiled, but it looked less genuine than usual. He was uncomfortable, and it was all my fault. I couldn't believe how badly I was screwing this up in such a short amount of time.

"You know what? Denver and I are going to check out the treehouse. Call us when lunch is ready." Everyone else could finish prepping the food. I took his hand and practically dragged him outside.

The treehouse Dad built for us kids had mostly been Parker and Clay's headquarters, with me as their insistent tag-along. But it still held a lot of good memories for me. Like the summer we put up a fake lemonade stand with signs directing customers to the backyard so we could pelt them with water balloons from above. Clay, ever the peacemaker, had decided it was only fair to leave a bucket with water balloons below the tree so they could hit us back. Best day ever.

"This is sick. I love it." Denver climbed up the ladder first and ducked his head in to have a look. The dust and cobwebs were always trying to claim the place, but Dad kept it clean and in good shape for when Raelyn came over. I was surprised she wasn't up here already.

I sat on the bench inside, leaving room for Denver, but he was too busy spider-monkeying across the rope bridge to get to the lookout tower. He really was like a little kid sometimes.

From this high up, I could see the street in front of the house and Clay's truck pulling to the curb. The pest. I knew he'd come.

Parker and Dad pulled in right after him. They must have all met up at the shop to check the alarm together. Denver ducked back in and sat next to me. "I never had anything like this as a kid. You're so lucky."

"We had some good times up here."

There was a unicorn sleeping bag on the floor, and Denver leaped down and stretched out on it, laying one arm across his face to block the sunlight shining in through the window. "I was up until four last night playing X-Box in my cousin's tournament. Do you mind if I rest my eyes for a little bit, you know, as long as we're hiding out from your relatives?"

I smiled. "Sure thing."

He turned, trying to get comfortable. "And yeah, your family's weird."

"You've only met half of them."

He gave me a thumbs up in return and was snoring within a minute.

CHAPTER 9

CLAY

It wouldn't be a Harwood family event if I didn't get spit-up on me at some point, and apparently today would be no exception.

"Burp him, please." Melissa handed Jax to me no less than four seconds after I walked in before following her mother-in-law to the kitchen to deal with a baking emergency. I possessed some sort of baby magic that had started with Raelyn. For a while, I was one of the few people who could hold her without causing her to cry.

"Hey, buddy." I sat on the edge of the couch and balanced Jax on my knee, gently patting his back until he burped like a trucker. He smiled big before a trail of milk leaked out of his mouth and onto the burp cloth below him. I thought I was in the clear until he waved one of his chubby arms around and managed to pick up a handful of spit-up from the burp cloth and glom it on the arm I was holding him with.

"Thanks, dude. Much appreciated."

Parker and John walked in and shook their heads at the sight of me. They both loved Jax, but neither were great with babies except to make faces at them and hand them off the second they yelled or smelled.

"Where's everyone else?" John asked me. "Lauren's truck is here."

"I've only seen Melissa and Charlotte. I assume Connor's at the grill. He's much better at not burning stuff than the rest of us."

Parker made a face. "Lauren's probably off making out with her boyfriend somewhere. She always gets out of cooking."

The thought of her off making out with some guy who I knew wasn't her boyfriend caused my head to pulse, so I focused on the second part of what Parker had said. "She gets out of cooking because she can't cook."

"And why do you think that is?" Parker waved his arms out like a prosecutor making his case. "She does it on purpose. The same way she used to get out of taking out the garbage because she said the neighbor's dog growled at her through the fence."

John, looking bored with our argument, walked into the kitchen. Charlotte squealed, and John's chuckle followed, along with his deep baritone serenading her with his off-key version of an Elvis love song.

I couldn't help but smile. John and Charlotte were never shy about their exuberance in seeing each other.

Parker collapsed on the couch next to me. "I don't know why they have to make such a production of it."

"That's because you've never known someone you wanted in your arms every time you saw her."

"Um, what?"

I continued to pat Jax, reminding myself my secret was safe. If Parker hadn't figured out I'd been desperately pining for his sister for the past seven years, today would make no difference. Even so, I had an answer ready to throw him off the trail. "You forget I didn't grow up with that. I'm still not sure if my grandparents even like each other."

Parker sniffed. "I'm sure they do. They've spent fifty years together."

"They have common goals and a mutual distrust of

strangers. That's not love, that's being practical."

I could tell Parker didn't agree with me, but then, I didn't agree with his assessment of his parents either. It was better to leave each other to our biases.

Melissa hurried back in, arms outstretched to take Jax from me. "I'm sorry, Clay. I didn't mean to leave him with you for so long. Oh, and Connor is asking for you two. He said if he has to sweat all over a grill, you should too."

"And yet he didn't ask for Lauren. Typical."

"Give it a rest, Parker." I frogged him in the leg and took off before he could get me back.

Outside, I got to work arranging the backyard tables and chairs according to Charlotte's directions while Parker and Connor argued over whether the steaks were done or not. Lauren was nowhere in sight, but I had a feeling that had nothing to do with cooking and everything to do with hiding her not-boyfriend from the family. For someone she was only casually dating, she sure was worried about what he might think.

Raelyn tugged on the bottom of my shirt. She had a kickball tucked under her arm that was almost as big as she was. "Will you play ball with me, Clay?"

"Well, of course, you little rag-a-muffin. I was wondering when you'd come say hi." I stole the kickball from her and ran off, knowing she'd follow.

We kicked it back and forth in the grass under the treehouse until Melissa called for her to come and go potty and wash her hands before lunch, which of course, Raelyn did not want to do. Melissa ended up chasing her down and carrying her into the house like a screaming sack of potatoes.

John headed my way with a deep frown, and a sense of foreboding settled over me. We hadn't talked about Lauren since he'd asked me to come today, and I had a feeling that was what he wanted to talk about now.

He glanced around, as if afraid we'd be overheard. "Have you seen Lauren yet? I want to see this guy who's so special I'm not allowed to meet him."

"Are you surprised?"

John frowned. "What's that supposed to mean?"

"You told her she could get out of the Idaho trip if she brought him today. She's not going to take that without making you sweat a little. That's how you Harwoods are, am I right?"

John blew out a frustrated breath. "I guess."

"She told me not to come today."

"Does she know I asked you to be here?"

"No. And let's pretend that conversation never happened. I can't do these little favors for you, John. You're abusing your boss privileges."

"I suppose I am. Sorry, Clay."

He walked off, and I let out a sigh of relief. He'd try again, no doubt, but I felt better for telling him anyway. I kicked the ball up from the bottom of my shoe and bounced it on my knee. I'd always sucked at soccer, but Parker and I had perfected the trick shots that made us look better than we were.

There was a sudden creak overhead, and I glanced up at the treehouse, just as Lauren's head popped out the window. She looked as mad as a hornet. If she'd overheard our conversation just now, I was so dead.

"You have some explaining to do, Clay."

Yep, she definitely heard. On instinct, I backed up, but she came down the ladder fast, running at me the second she hit the ground. I took off, throwing the kickball behind me to slow her down. I was almost to the white vinyl fence that separated their property from the neighbors, prepared to hop over it in one bound, but she caught me around the waist and took me to the grass, sitting on my back for good measure. I craned my neck around and took in her look of angry satisfaction.

"This isn't fair. I'm not going to wrestle you, Lauren."

"You're only saying that because you lost."

I rested my chin on my arms and sighed. "Fine. Say your piece."

"What favors?"

"I don't know what you're talking about."

She reached down and tickled my sides, and I immediately jumped in response, almost rolling over to tackle her and make her stop before my better judgment kicked in. I could not wrestle with Lauren. Not ever. My only choice was surrender.

"Okay, okay. I'll talk."

"What favors have you been doing for my dad?"

"I cancelled his appointment with the dermatologist for him and rescheduled it." Which was true. Charlotte would have lectured him about missing it again, so he asked me to do it.

"You know that's not what I'm talking about. You told my dad no more little favors just now. What did you mean?" She slid off me and sat in the grass, looking much more serious. "Please, Clay."

Her sad brown eyes did me in. And my goose was cooked anyway. There was nothing for it but the truth. "He asked me to come today and give him my opinion on your guy."

"And you've done this before?" She looked so hurt and vulnerable, that I reached out and gripped her ankle, holding it like I might have held her hand if I could.

"I've never talked to your dad about your dating life before this week, I swear."

"Then why now?"

"I guess because he noticed how good I am at making fun of..."

"My boyfriends? And he thinks I broke up with them because of things you said? You wish you held that kind of power over me, Clay."

"I've never held any power over you. Trust me, I know."

Our eyes met and something potent passed between us. Something I shouldn't have allowed.

"Lauren?"

We glanced over at the guy walking towards us who I could only assume was Denver. I released her ankle and jumped to my feet, brushing off the grass.

He put out his hand to shake mine. "You must be one of

Lauren's brothers. I'm Denver."

"Clay."

Lauren got to her feet and kicked at the ground. "Clay is like the extra brother I never wanted."

Denver laughed. "Well, that's rude."

"No, I mean, he's a neighbor kid who refused to go home. He's best friends with my brother."

"Oh, cool." Denver glanced behind us at the back porch where the O'Dells and the rest of Lauren's family were standing, watching us with rapt attention. "Um, your mom says lunch is ready, Lauren."

CHAPTER 10

LAUREN

The O'Dells had shown up just in time to make things extra awkward. Our life-long neighbors, Patty and Roger, had always teased Clay and I about how we were meant to end up together, and like the rest of their conspiracy theories, they'd convinced absolutely no one in the past. Well, I was secretly in agreement with them on the Roswell cover-up thing.

Patty put her hands to her cheeks and looked at Clay and me as if we had just fulfilled all her day-time soap opera fantasies. "Aren't the two of you adorable? Absolutely adorable. Like I always say—" She cut off when she saw Denver standing next to me and blinked. "That uh, you young people are the cutest. Who's this?"

"This is Denver. So, lunch is ready?"

I grabbed Denver's hand and went to claim our seats at the table. Dad came around and shook Denver's hand before sitting next to him and politely asking him about sports teams and hobbies and lots of totally normal things that made me suspicious. Dad never made small talk.

It was because he knew I'd overheard him talking to Clay and he wanted to make up for it. That was all. I took a long drink of lemonade before reaching out for Jax. My appetite had gone dormant, and I knew Melissa would relish the chance to eat with both hands. She handed him over like I'd volunteered as tribute for her in the Hunger Games.

It wasn't just my dad. The whole family was super nice to Denver during the meal, and that only made me feel worse. It didn't matter. Denver was already breaking up with me, or un-dating me, or whatever you did when you went on a handful of dates with a person and decided it was better to not call again.

I could see it in his body language, in the way he studied Clay when he thought no one else was looking. It didn't stop Denver from eating steak. I think he ate three, along with two baked potatoes and a whole plate of salad. I almost smiled. Going out to eat with him had always been fun. He made food an event, a concept I could really get behind. And now it was all over. Back to meeting guys who thought it was romantic to text and ask for sexy pictures. I had an image of a warthog on my phone for just such occasions before I blocked their numbers.

"What happened with the alarm going off?" I asked Parker, realizing I wasn't being a part of the conversation as much as I should be. I took my slice of key lime pie from Mom without meeting her eyes. She'd be able to read me if I looked at her too closely, and I wasn't ready for that. I'd cry with her later, when I knew exactly what it was that made me want to cry.

"Nothing. A cottontail probably tripped it going through the fence." Parker glanced from me, to Clay, to Denver, and back again, and I inwardly flinched. There was a curiosity there, a wariness. Clay was *his* friend, not mine. I was getting in the way of Parker's perfectly ordered life, messing things up. As the middle kid, Parker was naturally territorial. And as the baby, I was the one who got everything. Or so he thought.

But I wasn't taking anything from Parker. Not this time. He was seeing something that wasn't there, the way the O'Dells saw Elvis as alive and kicking and Bigfoot hiding in the woods, leaving trails of DNA for the Travel Channel to capitalize on.

Yeah, maybe Clay found me attractive, but only enough to tease when nobody else was around to see it. I swallowed the lump in my throat and told myself I didn't care.

"This key lime pie is amazing." Denver shook his head. "Thanks so much, Mrs. H."

Mom smiled. I don't think anyone had ever called her that, and I could tell she liked it.

"When will the bucket truck be ready to rent out?" Dad asked Clay.

They went back and forth over repair issues, and I tuned them out until Denver nudged my arm. "Clay works with you?"

"Yep."

"I see."

I'm sure he did. Denver was a lot of things, but stupid was not one of them.

"Are you ready?" I asked, noticing his empty pie plate. He hadn't left a crumb.

We said our goodbyes right there at the table, and I took our two dessert plates into the kitchen to rinse before we walked out. Denver followed me to my truck and opened my door for me before going around and getting in the passenger side. He pulled out his phone and stared at it for several minutes while I drove.

I actually jumped when he finally spoke. "It's really hard to read you, Lauren. And I'm good with just hanging out, but not if you're secretly hooking up with some guy from work on the side. That's too complicated for me."

"I'm not... I've never hooked up with anyone." I thought he knew that about me, even though I'd never come out and said it.

He put his phone down and looked at me for several beats. "And I'm so good with that. Good for you. But that dude's not your brother. I was relieved when you said he wasn't. There was like, so much sexual tension there when I walked up."

I blinked, trying to focus on the road. "I'm sorry. I just put you through the worst date ever. You were such a good sport, and I made a fool of myself." I pulled at my collar, knowing my apology didn't even begin to cut it. I turned and caught Denver smiling at me.

"They don't know, do they? Your family?"

"Know what?"

"That you and Clay have somethin-somethin going on." He saw my look and immediately corrected himself. "That you two wish you had somethin-somethin going on."

I let out a huge sigh. "I don't think they know. But nothing's happened with me and Clay. Ever."

"Nothing?"

"You don't want to hear this, Denver."

"Yeah, I do. I just got friend-zoned. So no more giving me the vault every time I ask about your life."

He still wanted to be friends with me? I didn't know whether to be flattered or offended. I hadn't broken his heart. Not even a little bit. In fact, I had a feeling he had a list of girls to call when he got home. I wished I could conjure up just a little bit of jealousy over that, but I felt only disappointment.

"Nothing is going to happen between me and Clay. We work together, and he's my brother's best friend. They've always had each other's backs. If Clay had to pick, he'd choose his friendship with my brother over a relationship with me all day, every day. And that includes giving me a hard time, because that's what Parker likes to do."

"That's messed up."

"Yeah. I think Clay could be a decent guy if he tried, but he doesn't. I'm at peace with that."

"No, you're not."

"No, I'm not." I smiled.

We'd reached Denver's house, the one he shared with several roommates. He leaned over and gave me a hug before hopping out and slamming the passenger door. I would have thought he was angry with me if I wasn't already familiar with his passion for slamming doors to make sure they shut. The truck window was down, and he leaned in, resting his arms on the door frame. "I'll call you, sometime. I don't know when."

"Okay." I loved his honesty. Everything with Denver was open and real. I'd never get that with anyone else, least of all Clay, and that was why my mission when I returned to my parents' house was damage control. When I was done, not only would Clay be convinced I was indifferent to him, but everyone else would be, too.

CHAPTER 11

CLAY

Charlotte handed me two slices of her key lime pie covered in plastic wrap on a paper plate. "For your grandparents."

She knew it would be easier if I had something to bring, something that gave purpose to my visit. Not that I was going over there on a whim. I'd called them last week to let them know when I'd come see them. You didn't show up to my grandparent's house unannounced. The Publisher's Clearing House Sweepstakes people would've been in for a surprise if they ever knocked on their door. They'd have to use that oversized check as a shield against my grandmother's broom whacking them off her porch.

"Do you want me to go with?" Parker asked.

"Nah." I didn't mind the awkwardness if I didn't have an audience. Besides, Parker had Lauren-related questions for me, and I didn't have it in me to deflect them properly right now. He wasn't the only one. If it wasn't for Patty and Roger O'Dell, I'd be in the middle of a Harwood inquisition. Bless those two odd souls and their endless speculation on whether the government was actively keeping people from finding the Lost Dutchman Gold Mine.

Every time John tried to get up and excuse himself, Patty

would reach out and pull him back down into his seat. Nobody was finished with a conversation without her say-so.

"You're coming back though, right?" Parker picked up one of Jax's burp cloths from the couch seat with two fingers before sitting down. He usually didn't stay this long, but Charlotte was about to hem a pair of pants for him, so he was stuck until then. I had a feeling he'd also be leaving with a haircut and enough leftovers to last him a week. Parker was in complete denial about how good Charlotte was to him.

"Um, yeah. I'll come back." I walked down the street, leaving my truck in front of the Harwoods' house.

Grandma answered when I knocked. "Hello, Clayton. Come in." She stepped aside so I could walk into the foyer. The familiar smell of Windex and rose potpourri tickled my nose. Even the way the light filtered through the blinds was familiar. This was home and not home, all at the same time. I'd been afraid of this front room when I was little. I think it was the ticking clock and the Nutcracker doll on the mantle with his bared teeth and wild, white hair puffing out under his cap. If he'd started out as a Christmas decoration, the idea was lost on Grandma. He stood at creepy attention all year long.

I ended my staring contest with the doll and turned to Grandma. "I brought you some pie from the Harwoods."

"Thank you, I'll put this in the fridge." She hurried off with it, leaving me alone for the moment.

I took the opportunity to pick up the framed picture of my mom from the side table and study it. Her life had never been a mystery to me, and I was grateful for that. Parker had spent so much of his childhood speculating about his mom and why no one would talk about her. We were preteens before Parker found out the whole truth, that she'd run off with a man she'd known only a few months. They'd secretly dated while she was pregnant with Parker, and she left for good shortly after he was born. The shock of hearing it was permanently seared in me. I couldn't imagine the pain for John or his boys.

I studied my mom's dark blue eyes, so much like mine. She

had dropped out of college and returned home pregnant with me. Leukemia took her a few months after my first birthday. She never would say who my father was. Grandma had explained these things to me over and over when I was little, in that matter-of-fact way of hers. For all their faults, my grandparents had never made me feel like a burden or a secret. I was theirs to take care of. It was their duty, just like it was mine to help them now with whatever they needed.

Grandpa shuffled in, his bald head shining like a newly polished bowling ball. "Hello, Clayton. How is work?"

"Good, Grandpa. Would you like to see the bucket truck I've been working on?"

He shrugged. "Okay. Let me find my glasses." He came back with his reading glasses and Grandma trailing behind, and they both studied my photos, giving appropriate sounds of approval, though I knew neither of them really cared about what we were looking at.

Then we sat, and the clock ticked, and the Nutcracker leered, and I asked them questions about the garden, and the neighbors, and the news to keep the conversation going, until Grandma stood and clasped her hands together. "Let me get your coupons before you go."

She clipped every coupon from the junk mail each week, even the ones she knew she wouldn't use. Grandpa was thrifty in other ways. He bought whole milk and watered it down, keeping it in several pitchers in the fridge.

In rebellion, my fridge always had pure, unadulterated whole milk, and I felt luxurious every time I drank it. Grandpa would never know.

Grandma came back with an envelope and pulled out the coupons from inside. "Do you eat at that Chinese restaurant on Seventh Street?"

"Uh, no." It did no good to lie. Grandma had a built in truth detector that never failed.

"What about the dry cleaners? This is for twenty-percent off."

"I don't use the dry cleaners much, Grandma. Why don't you use that one?"

She shook her head. "No. I won't use it either." She ripped that coupon in half and stuck it in the back of the stack.

We went through the rest of the coupons like this before she handed them to me, making me promise to use them.

I left with a lighter heart, but an ache in the back of my neck I recognized as my stress spot. My grandparents were my family, but the Harwoods were my heart. They were the people who taught me to love, to fight and forgive, to tease, and to let my guard down. They knew everything about me with one very large exception. How I felt about Lauren.

I closed my eyes. What was I supposed to do about her?

Nothing. Absolutely nothing. At least around her family. It was what I'd always done in the past. It couldn't fail me now. I wouldn't talk to Lauren any differently, and if anyone asked about us, I'd pretend I didn't know what they were talking about. Today made no difference.

I stopped at my truck and put Grandma's coupons in the console, knowing I'd have to use at least one of them. She'd interrogate me about them the next time I came to mow the lawn. A free ice cream cone from McDonald's wasn't the worst thing ever.

"Hey, Olsen. You're not allowed to leave yet."

Startled by Lauren's sudden presence, I hit my head on the frame of my truck and cussed. "I wasn't trying to leave, Lauren. Though now I think I should. Where's your truck?" If I'd known she was coming back, I certainly wouldn't have stayed. Today had been enough of a disaster.

She pointed to the neighbor's RV parked on the street. "I'm on the other side of this monster. The Binghams just got home from their trip to Durango."

"Good for them. I'll see you later." I got into my truck, but she climbed up on the running board before I could shut the door.

She had to stop invading my space like this. I could see every little freckle across her cheeks, the flecks of gold in her brown eyes, the little blonde hairs at the top of her forehead that danced, refusing to be smooth and sleek. And I noticed her lips. I always noticed her lips. She'd recently applied lip gloss. Strawberry scented if I wasn't mistaken.

"What do you want?" I crossed my arms and glanced behind her to make sure no one was watching us through the front window.

"I'm confronting my dad about Denver and every other guy I've dated or will date, and I need you there to witness it."

"I'm sorry about Denver." The words slipped out before I had a chance to rethink them.

Her eyes flashed. "No you're not. Mission accomplished, right? He's thoroughly scared off. He's not even sort of my boyfriend anymore."

That did make me just a little bit happy, and she must have seen it in my face. "You're the worst, Clay. Never mind. You're free to go."

It took everything in me to let her stalk off, believing I enjoyed ruining her life. Not that I thought it was ruined. Denver was not the guy for her. He was a placeholder. A dot in her history she'd barely remember years from now. I'd vowed long ago to concede my game the day she found a guy worthy of her. Today was not that day.

I let her go inside before getting out and locking up my truck. The Clay she knew wouldn't listen when she said I was free to go.

CHAPTER 12

LAUREN

I breathed deeply before going inside my parents' house. Despite what I'd just told Clay, I wasn't planning on yelling at anyone. That was the fastest way to make sure my dad didn't listen to me. But it was time to confront him about how he'd blackmailed me into bringing Denver, and why.

Everyone was in the front room to witness the mighty event of Parker getting a haircut. Perfect. I wouldn't even have to round them all up.

I cleared my throat. "So, we need to talk about what just happened. Dad told Clay to come check out my boyfriend and cause trouble today."

Everyone turned to look at me, except for Raelyn, who was mesmerized by a computer tablet, and Parker, who was having the back of his neck shaved.

Dad's face turned red. "That's an exaggeration, and you know it."

"Is it?"

Parker scoffed. "Cause trouble? If I recall, Clay didn't take you to the ground and sit on you." I could hear the smile in his voice. He loved when I acted impulsively. Especially since I often accused him of doing the same thing.

"I forgot Denver might not see it as a brother-sister sort of interaction. Half the time, I don't remember Clay's not blood."

I was getting nods. Yes! I could do this.

The door behind me creaked open, and I took a deep breath. Clay. My annoying almost-brother. He couldn't be anything else to me. My happiness depended on it. I allowed myself a quick glance before moving out of the way so he could go sit on the couch.

Mom put the clippers down and folded her arms. "John, did you tell Clay to come cause trouble today? And what made you think he could cause trouble? This is our Clay." She smiled down at him like he was her sweet little boy who could do no wrong. I swear she loved him more than me, but unlike Parker, I wasn't bitter about it. My mom had enough love for us, the rainforests, all the orphans in the world, and every neighbor kid who had ever hit her up for extortion in the name of school fundraisers.

Clay cleared his throat. "He asked me to come and form an opinion about Denver. Sorry, Lauren."

"Whatever. Apology accepted. This is about my dad, not you." With that dismissal, I turned to Dad. "Did you tell Parker you made me choose between going to Idaho and bringing Denver here today?"

Parker looked up at me in surprise, and for the first time in a long time, I saw admiration there. I'd chosen his happiness over mine and hadn't even rubbed it in his face. But that I'd had to do it at all was what we needed to talk about.

"Dad, you have to let me grow up. There's no need for a boyfriend intervention, not now, not ever. If I need help, I will ask. I promise. But I can't learn from my mistakes if you're constantly trying to prevent them."

There was a long thoughtful silence before Dad nodded, clapping his hands down at his sides. "I didn't realize I was doing that. I'm sorry. I actually think Denver's not a bad guy."

"Me either. But he just wants to be friends now, so you can take the tracker off his car and stop bugging his house."

"Ha, ha. Very funny." He held his arms out for a hug, and I

moved to give him one. Dad smelled like barbeque and my childhood. I loved him despite thinking he was the most infuriating person on the planet. Okay, in the top three. Clay and Parker were up there too.

Dad released me and looked over my head at the rest of the room. "Maybe this is a good time to mention that Mom and I have been talking. We think it's time we restructure the company so we have a hand-off legally in place when the time comes. Parker and Lauren, we want to leave the company to you."

What? I turned to see Clay's surprised expression and Parker's wary one. Knowing Parker, this was something he'd probably thought a lot about and formed an opinion on long before we'd reached this day. I wasn't sure how I felt yet.

"Not me?" Connor asked with a twinkle in his eye. He'd learned early on that working with Dad was the fastest way to ruin their relationship. And thanks to his successful dental practice, he didn't need the money.

Dad reached out and took Mom's hand. "We'll talk more about it another day. Your mother doesn't want too much shop talk when we're all together like this."

"Split in half?" Parker asked. "And a partnership-at-will or a limited partnership?"

"Parker," Dad warned. "We'll get into that. And also discuss what happens in the case of death or divorce. Talking about Lauren dating made me think of it, but there will be plenty of time to hash all that all out."

My dating life made him think of death and divorce? I met Clay's eyes and knew he was thinking the same thing. My dad must've had all sorts of worst-case-scenarios rolling through his head when it came to me. But he forgot to mention Stockholm syndrome, avalanches, alien invasions, and the possibility that I might be replaced by a robot wife. Faith Hill was in a movie where that happened, right?

"Sounds great, Dad." I'd only just returned, but it was best if we broke up this little party before Parker said something that spoiled my dad's happiness in sharing it with us. "I'm headed home. See, ya'll tomorrow."

Despite Mom's protests, I turned and escaped out the front door, hurrying to my truck. Owning the business? I should be excited, and in theory I was. But in reality? It sounded like a lot more trouble than resenting my Dad's control over everything.

CHAPTER 13

CLAY

I was happy for Parker and Lauren. Over the moon happy for them. They were family. I was not. I would not be one of those resentful long-time employees who tried to undermine things from the inside out, who let hurt feelings canker until all I saw was my own insecurities and jealousy. John already paid me more than I'd make anywhere else. He had paid for all of my certifications and kept me up-to-date on new ones. Yes, I had a business degree in addition to being a master mechanic, but that didn't mean I needed to own my own company. Not at twenty-five.

I think what was giving me hives was the thought of Parker and Lauren trying to negotiate that world without me as a buffer. I now had less clout to tell them when they were wrong because… technically they'd be my bosses.

All these thoughts were running through my head, and I couldn't let any of it show while I was sitting here with everyone. Well, everyone except Lauren. I wanted to bolt, too. But if I did, I was afraid someone would suspect what I was feeling.

So I chatted with Connor and Melissa about the Phoenix

Suns and their recent trades and the upcoming season. I was what I would call a mild basketball fan, while they were slightly below rabid, where they had season tickets, and mentioning the L.A. Lakers in a positive way around them was a great way to start a fight.

Charlotte finished with Parker's haircut and brushed off his shoulders before shooing him away so she could clean up the mess. I helped her carefully pick up the four corners of the drop cloth she'd used to catch all the hair and then offered to take it outside and shake it off.

The street was quiet. Not so much as a leaf moved on the trees in the yard. I'd gather my things and go. I had a whole season of Pawn Shop Warriors I hadn't watched yet. Sometimes it was ridiculous what was trending on Netflix. I had a load of socks and T-shirts in the dryer that would not sort themselves. Yep, my life was pretty darn exciting.

Back inside, Charlotte took the drop cloth from me and handed me a glass dish with a matching plastic lid. "This is Lauren's, and it's the third time she's forgotten to take it on her way out. Parker's refusing to stop by and bring it to her."

"She doesn't even want it," Parker hollered from the kitchen. "Why do you think she left it here? She doesn't cook. Just keep it."

Charlotte rolled her eyes. "Anyway, you live close to her. When you go, will you drop this off to her?"

"Of course." Anything for Charlotte. This had nothing at all to do with seeing Lauren again tonight. Because I didn't want that. No, I did not. I could just leave it on her doorstep with a note sure to tick her off.

I took the glass dish, waved goodbye to everyone, and whistled on the way to my truck. I wasn't feeling relaxed, but there was power in acting relaxed while everything inside you churned like butter. All my life I'd been an outsider looking in on all the things that mattered most. Family, career, love. Someday, I'd get it all figured out. It didn't have to be right now.

I was glad the status quo had been reaffirmed. If Parker was fine with me dropping a dish off to his sister, he obviously didn't suspect that there was anything going on between us. And there wasn't. Crisis averted.

I pulled into Lauren's apartment complex and parked before jogging up the stairs to her apartment. Lauren's red-headed roommate was standing on her tiptoes attempting to hang a spring wreath on the door. For anyone else, the job would have taken five seconds tops, but she kept turning it one way or another and then stepping back to study it, as if some flowery angles were better than others. Maybe they were. I stomped my feet harder to alert her to my presence.

She turned and grinned very big when she saw me. "Clay, right?"

"Yep." I held out the dish. "Will you give this to Lauren?"

"Give it to her yourself." Suddenly satisfied with the wreath placement, she opened the door and gestured for me to come inside.

I'm not sure what I expected to see Lauren doing after a breakup. Eating ice cream, burning love tokens, crying. But no, she was sitting on the floor putting on running shoes with her earbuds in, singing off-key to a *Shadow Behind the Sun* song. She did a combination grunge-rock head bob and air guitar move, obviously psyching herself up for a good workout.

I stepped into her line of vision before we reached blackmail level, where she'd pay me a million dollars to never tell anyone what I'd just witnessed.

Lauren startled, landing back on her hands before pulling out her earbuds. "What are you doing here?" She turned to look at her roommate. "Jenny Lynn Baker, why is he here?"

Jenny rolled her eyes. "She's normally nicer than this."

"I feel honored knowing I bring out the worst in her." I held out the dish from Lauren's mom with my note taped on top. I had been planning for her to read it when I wasn't in grabbing distance.

But no. She took the pan and ripped off the note, unfolding it and reading it to herself before a hint of a smile played across her face. I'd initially planned to go with a dig at her lack of cooking skills, but that was Parker's idea of a joke so I just wrote: *Consider this another favor owed. I accept cookies.*

There was a long silence, and then Jenny clapped her hands together and tucked them under her chin. "I just forgot I have to run an errand." She grabbed her keys off the hook by the door and escaped before we could react, making it pretty clear she'd made up an excuse to leave us alone together. Maybe she lived in mortal fear of awkward pauses.

I scrambled for a conversation thread. "Going running?"

"Yep." Lauren ran her hands over the top of her hair, messing up her ponytail before she pulled out the rubber band and fixed it. Her legs looked especially long and shapely in the black leggings she was wearing, but I only allowed myself a quick glance.

"Where do you go?" I asked.

She shook her head. "Nope. It's my spot. I don't want you showing up there and ruining it."

I crossed my arms, channeling an attitude of deep offense. "How would I ruin it?"

"With your presence. I thought that was obvious." She got to her feet and moved to the kitchen, grabbing a water bottle off the counter. "Time to go, intruder."

She opened her door for me and gestured for me to leave, which I did. I wasn't nearly as annoying as she thought I was.

"I bet my running spot is better than yours." I threw it out casually as I started to walk away. Amble would be a better word. I was ambling away, which basically meant I'd taken about three slow steps.

"You think I'm tempted by that?" She followed me out and turned to lock her door.

"Maybe. Does your spot have hurdles you can jump over, just for the fun of it?"

"Are you hoping for an invitation so you can tag along with me?"

I made a face. "No. I'm trying to get *you* to tag along with *me*. Because my running spot is better than yours."

"Because of the hurdles?" She shook her head, trying not to laugh before looking me up and down. "Are you sure you're up for that? I don't think you should attempt to leap over hurdles in jeans. Unless you'd like to sing soprano from now on. And let me just say, I'd be okay with that. I fully support you in your choices."

"I'll be fine. My jeans are relaxed, unlike those uptight ones your boyfriend was wearing today."

Her eyes narrowed.

"Too soon. Sorry."

She took off past me down the corridor to the stairs, making her keys jingle in her hand.

"So, is that a yes?"

"To what?" she offered over her shoulder.

"To check out my running spot. This is a limited time offer. If you reject me, I'll go home and eat Oreos while lying on a pile of clean laundry I'm not folding and watch TV. My fitness and life skill goals will be completely wasted for the day. All because you hate me."

"I don't hate you. Mostly." She reached the bottom of the stairs and let out a long, exasperated breath. "Okay, let's be real here for a second. I know I have long legs, but I'm a slow runner. Like fifteen-minute-mile slow. And my face gets all blotchy and red. I also keep tissues in my pocket because sometimes my nose runs when I'm breathing hard. Still want to flirt it up with me?"

"I want to be friends. We're adults now. Isn't it about time?" It was time. For once, I wasn't joking. Something had to change, even if it was just for today. I wanted to be around her as much as she'd let me, and I was tired of fighting that instinct.

She shrugged. "I'll follow you to your special running spot. We'll see about the friend thing." There was some bitterness clinging to the word 'friend,' but I'd take the slightly wilted olive branch she was offering and go with it.

I got in my truck and drove slowly enough that there was no

way she could claim she got lost on our way to the middle school. And I prayed the hurdles were still set up. They were left out more often than not. They really did make running more fun. There was something about rounding the track and knowing you could go all gazelle for thirty seconds that was extra motivating.

Perfect. They were still there, and Lauren was right behind me. She pulled into a parking spot about a hundred yards away, as if my truck had a disease she didn't want to catch. But at least she came. I quickly changed into the running shorts I kept in my gym bag from back when I had a gym membership. The jeans thing was a bluff. She was right. There was no way I'd be jumping hurdles in jeans.

I got out in my socks, holding my Nikes, and sat down in the grass to put them back on. I'd almost worn boots today too. That would have been a deal breaker.

Lauren plopped down next to me and rested her arms across her legs. "I was looking forward to watching you split your jeans when you jumped hurdles."

"I bet you were."

She shoved my arm. "John should be leaving the company to you, too, you know. You're as much family as the rest of us."

Where had that come from? "No, I'm not." I didn't want to get into it with her. For some reason, hearing her say it was making my throat want to close off. I was filled with elation at her acknowledgement of what I'd never be free to say, but the anger and frustration kicked in too, and I wouldn't go down that road again, not tonight. I'd already stuffed those feelings down where they couldn't bother me. I wanted them to stay there.

I jumped to my feet and walked over to the track, not looking back to see if she planned to follow, wind-milling my arms in a show of stretching out, although when I ran alone I never stretched first.

Lauren's feet came plodding up from behind, and when she passed me up and turned to face me, I couldn't help laughing. Her face was full-on grouch. As much as she hated being teased, being ignored was way worse in her book.

I'd dismissed her when she thought she was being thoughtful and inclusive. All that good-intentioned crap that led to unintended consequences. Bringing up something that couldn't be changed was not helpful. Not to me, not to anybody.

"You've worked at Sun Valley longer than me, and just as long as Parker."

Great, she wanted to keep talking about it. "So has Herbert. By those rules, shouldn't he get a cut too?"

She stopped trying to walk backwards and fell in step next to me. "Don't be dismissive of who you are, Clay. You're one of us. Herbert's an old guy who happens to know a lot about engines and is so set in his ways he'd still show up even if we tried to fire him. And if you recall, John's tried. It's easier to just let Herbert come and occasionally screw stuff up."

"I don't need validation for who I am. I'm not worried about this, so please stop trying to create a problem where there isn't one."

"I'm not creating a problem. You're afraid to say something."

The pain in my neck had returned, caused by my other pain in the neck. I took Lauren's arm and turned her towards me, letting her see the frustration coursing through me. "Yes, I'm afraid. I'm afraid you'll say something and make this awkward for me. We're talking about my career, and you can't micromanage it. You don't get a say in it just because you want to call me your brother when it's convenient for you."

Her mouth dropped open and she huffed a little. "It's not micromanaging to point out the obvious."

There was only one way to make her shut up about this. Okay, two ways, and I wasn't about to kiss her. This was one of the few times I wasn't tempted. I was that irritated. So, I defaulted to the one I did best.

I reached out and tucked a lock of her hair back behind her ear that had come loose. "I was already aware your skin gets red and blotchy when you exercise. Especially your neck. It happens when you get mad at me too, like right now. I don't get under your skin. I get on your skin."

Her lips pinched together, and I took that cue to start running. This time I wouldn't let her catch me. The hurdles were coming up. Even better. I imagined her zig-zagging around them to keep up with me and a mad laugh burst out.

"Clay!"

Oh, good. She'd heard me laughing. I leaped over the first hurdle. Amazing. The best feeling ever. Being a middle school and not a high school track, the hurdles were shorter. I got great height over the second and third ones. Seven more to go.

I made the mistake of looking back at her, and the top of my foot connected with the bar of the forth hurdle. Everything went wrong from there. I was in the air, and then I was down on the ground, one with the rubberized asphalt. It must have looked epic.

"Clay?" Lauren ran and knelt beside me, her fingers moving over my arms and legs and head, like a butterfly not sure where to land.

I groaned and laid my face against the warm track. "Karma is on top of things, as usual."

She snort laughed, the kind that sneaks out when you're desperately trying to hold it in. "Are you okay?" She laid down next to me and turned her head so we were eye to eye.

"Never been better. I'm excellent." I was pretty sure I had a skinned knee and elbow, but all things considered, the worst of it was my bruised ego.

"I'm starting to see why this running spot of yours is so special." She smiled, looking especially pleased with herself.

"Anything for you, Lauren. I'm glad you're enjoying this."

"I really am." She reached out and ruffled my hair. "They're called hurdles, but I don't think you're supposed to hurtle yourself over them."

"How long have you been holding onto that gem?"

"About thirty seconds. You ready to get up and actually do some running with me? This might be the last really nice weekend before it gets too hot to run outside, and I hate treadmills."

"I'm ready." I lifted myself up and flipped my legs around to inspect them. A little bit of road rash on one knee. Nothing a good shower couldn't take care of.

She got to her feet and held a hand out to help me up. I imagined tugging on it and letting her land right back down with me. Holding her. Making her laugh. Kissing her lower lip and watching her eyes flutter closed. I tucked those images away in a practiced compartmentalizing of my feelings and let her help me to my feet. Friends didn't imagine crossing boundaries that weren't welcome.

She set the pace, which was, as she'd warned, really slow. But I didn't care about a good workout, and I'd taken my teasing far enough. Instead, I just listened.

I learned more about her in the next half-hour than I had in several years of catching bits and pieces. Lauren had problems with insomnia and bought used paperbacks to read when she couldn't sleep. Reading on her phone kept her up. She worried about her roommate because some guy at work had backed out of a date with her for mysterious reasons. Most of her stories involved Jenny. The two of them had been roommates for almost a year.

"Where did you meet Denver?" I asked, weaving through the hurdles as we came around the track again. We'd jumped over them on the first two go-rounds, but after that, we treated them like pathways.

She looked at me funny. "Why do you want to know that?"

"I don't know. I'm curious, I guess."

"I met him at a restaurant. I was with Jenny. It was crowded, with a long wait, and he and the friend he was with offered to share a table with us."

"Hmm."

"No jokes?"

"What's there to joke about? The dude's got game. I'm impressed."

Lauren slowed to a walk, and I matched her pace.

After a minute of silence she asked, "How come you don't date? Or do I just not hear about it?"

"I'm picky, I guess." I could practically feel her roll her eyes in reaction, but she was the one who asked. What did she expect me to say?

"And what's your type? What are you looking for?"

"Tall blondes with brown eyes. Feisty. Speedy in a truck but slower on foot." I turned, as if surprised to see her jogging next to me. "Oh, look. There's one right here."

She slapped me away good-naturedly, but I saw the question in her eyes. She didn't want to believe there was truth in my teasing, but she still… wondered. Good.

CHAPTER 14

LAUREN

The sun was setting, showing off with a blaze of pink and orange as only an Arizona sky could do. It was time to go. I hated how comfortable I felt with Clay, because I knew it wouldn't last. I could count on one hand the number of times it was just the two of us together, and things were different when other people were around. Parker would not be hearing about us hanging out together this afternoon. Not from me, and certainly not from Clay.

"Water break?" I asked, heading towards my truck.

Clay jogged over and jumped up into the bed of his truck where he kept a cooler with cold water bottles. The dude was prepared for anything, I'd give him that.

He came over and leaned against my truck door next to me, drinking water and staring at the sunset.

"So, where's your super-secret running spot?" he asked.

"Not telling." I knew he'd ask, and I had no intention of sharing, if for no other reason than because he wanted to know.

"That's fair. I'd hate to ruin it with my presence."

"How's your knee?" I leaned over to have a look. "I guess it is too hairy to throw a Band-Aid on there."

"You're calling my knees hairy?" He covered them up so I couldn't hurt them anymore with my insults.

"You called my neck red and blotchy."

"Your neck is beautiful in any color and you know it."

I looked away so he wouldn't see me smile. "Thank you, I guess."

His phone rang, and he gave a deep sigh when he checked the caller ID. Glancing at me, he finally flipped it around to show me it was my dad calling. He put his finger to his lips and answered.

"Hey John, what's up?"

"Hey, Clay. I wanted to pick your brain about something."

Clay glanced at me, and I knew he was nervous about where this was going. He hadn't taken it well when I'd brought up the company ownership thing.

"Go ahead." To his credit, Clay didn't move away from me. In fact, he shifted closer, leaning into me with his arm braced against my truck so I could hear better. Now I was the one feeling nervous. Clay smelled like grass and clean-scented deodorant and warm skin.

"It's about what Lauren said today."

Clay's eyes met mine and widened. "Okay."

"I can't stop her from meeting someone new, and after what she said I realize I shouldn't. But maybe I could introduce her to… I don't know. Someone decent. Someone I wouldn't mind having around. Someone safe."

I closed my eyes and gritted my teeth. The man hadn't learned anything. He'd listened and then taken all his controlling ways and channeled them in a new direction. I'd tell him exactly where he could stick his matchmaking. I moved to take the phone from Clay's hand, but he blocked me and wrapped his free arm around my waist, pinning my arms at my sides. I could have broken the hold he had on me, but then he would have moved away and I still wanted to hear.

"John, that sounds like the opposite of what she's asking for. Don't you want Lauren to trust you?"

"Of course I do. It's just, you remember what happened with Boyce."

"That was a long time ago. I don't think Lauren's planning to date anyone in the company again." Clay stared down, not meeting my eyes. He adjusted his hold on me, but didn't let go. In fact, I could have sworn his thumb caressed the edge of my wrist before settling again. I watched his eyes follow the curve of my neck from my earlobe down to my collar bone. "Did you have someone in mind?" he asked.

I thunked Clay in the chest with my forehead to let him know exactly what I thought of that question. Of course my dad had someone in mind. Why else would he call to get a second opinion?

"Well, there's a young man Melissa was telling me about. He just graduated from ASU, and she says he's church-going, doesn't party. And he's been too focused on his studies to date."

"Then let Melissa set them up." Clay finally met my eyes, his look full of sympathy.

"Oh, I will. I was just wondering if you could, I don't know, keep an eye on things at work. If she's determined to do her own thing, I'm afraid she'll pick someone at work just to spite me. Like date Evan or something."

"Evan has a girlfriend."

"See, this is exactly what I needed to know. I won't worry about Evan now."

"John, we can't have these kinds of conversations. Lauren will kill us both. I really need to go. I'll see you tomorrow, okay?"

"Okay. But I had one other thought."

Of course he did.

"Do you think you'd be up for a double date? If Melissa got her to go out with this young man, could you go with them and report back to me?"

"Report back to you? No, I can't do that."

"Nothing in depth. Just a thumbs up or thumbs down so I

don't worry. That's all I'm asking."

Clay sighed, blowing warm air across the side of my head. I gave a little nod, letting him know he could agree. My anger was building, and rather than shut this thing down, I wanted to know how far it would go. How much would my dad try to use Clay to check up on me?

"I can give you a thumbs up or thumbs down. But that's it. You need to let Lauren live her life without spying on her."

"I understand. Thanks for your help."

Clay hung up the phone and stuck it in his back pocket one-handed. Breathing deeply, he stared off in the distance. "Sorry."

Now that we didn't have the phone call to share, Clay still holding me held more and more meaning the longer he did it. And my anger was easier to deal with than an attraction that I didn't fully understand, on his side or mine.

I pulled away from him and walked away from the truck. "I'm having a hard time believing these conversations don't happen a lot. What is wrong with the two of you?"

"Lauren, I swear, before last week, we've never discussed your dating life. I have no idea why he's suddenly decided to use me as his confidant."

"So, this push for us to be friends? That doesn't have anything to do with him?"

The hurt in Clay's eyes told me I was over-reaching, going into conspiracy-theory territory, but was it so far-fetched? Dad would be all for it. Easier to hear my thoughts this way rather than asking me directly.

"I need to go." I waited for Clay to move away from my driver door and then got in without saying anything else. He watched me drive off, his arms folded, looking stoic.

I called Jenny as soon as I couldn't see Clay in my rearview mirror anymore.

"Lauren? You're supposed to check in with me when you go running. I was worried 'cause it's been like an hour."

"I was with Clay."

"Oh." She swooped the word, injecting all sorts of

expectation into it.

"Yeah, it was … I don't know. I'm feeling all sorts of things right now and they're having a boxing match in my head. My head hurts." My heart hurt. I knew I'd projected my anger at my dad on Clay, but I wasn't ready to remove it either. I still had to see both of them first thing in the morning, and I wasn't convinced they didn't talk about me more than Clay was willing to admit.

"Come home and I'll feed you. And you can tell me whatever parts you want to share. I'll try not to get too excited about it."

"Why do you like Clay so much?" I asked, feeling grateful and grumpy. "You barely know him."

"I like what he does to you. You sit up a little taller when he's around. You feel more."

"Right now I want to feel less."

"Feelings are good."

"Not these ones."

CHAPTER 15

CLAY

John was ruining my life. It was like he knew I wanted to try something with Lauren, even something as innocuous as friendship. I couldn't even have that.

Those gloomy thoughts had me dragging my feet into the shop on Monday morning. After changing into a jumpsuit, I immediately got to work on the Aichi bucket truck we'd brought back from Idaho. These things were highly sought after. They could fit in a space the size of a single parking spot, meaning construction crews didn't have to shut down traffic or disrupt businesses while they washed high-rise building windows or serviced cell towers. The sooner it was rental-ready, the sooner we could turn it into a money-making machine.

Parker sought me out not ten minutes into replacing the seal on the hydraulic pump. He looked like he had a secret practically bursting out of him.

"We had an ownership meeting early this morning."

"Well that's a first, unless you count John talking to himself while he idles in his truck."

Parker shifted his feet from side to side. "John got a valuation done on the company so he can issue stocks and give me and Lauren each twenty percent. Charlotte will have another twenty percent, and Dad stays the majority owner with forty. Eventually, when they want to retire, we'll buy them out."

Charlotte did the books when John first started out, and although she hadn't had a day-to-day hand in things for years, it made sense to include her in the ownership. Especially if it gave her as much say as Parker and Lauren. If I had to pick the most level-headed member of the Harwood family, it would definitely be Charlotte.

"How are you feeling about all of it?" I asked, watching Parker's face.

He shrugged. "I feel like I should be happier about it, but we spent the last part of the meeting doing what we always do. I say something I think should change, Lauren disagrees on how we should go about it, and Dad gives us a verbal pat on the head and goes off to do whatever he already planned on."

"You're twenty-five, Parker. Give this some time."

He slugged me in the shoulder. "You sound like an old man. Like, all the time. And you look like an old man. Even your pants are high-water. Why are you wearing white socks with black shoes?"

"These aren't high-water. I'm squatting down." I stood to prove I was right, but my coveralls only hit my ankles. Dang it. I'd grabbed the wrong jumpsuit from the stacks. We had them professionally cleaned along with the rags to get out things like oil and brake fluid.

"Looking good, Clay," Evan said, giving me a low whistle. He came over to hover, and I ignored the two of them and went back to working. Their conversation was just background noise.

Evan nudged my shoulder after a few minutes. "You coming?"

"To what?"

"My house tonight. You haven't listened to a word I've said, have you?"

"Give me the short version," I said. Evan should be used to people ignoring him. He never shut up.

"My girlfriend is out of town, and we're playing Madden NFL

on my PlayStation. It will be a lot more fun than hanging out here all night."

"Okay, whatever." It wasn't like I had other plans on a Monday night. "Now, you two go get work done and leave me alone."

"See you at seven." Evan wandered off to go find other people to bother.

Parker left me a few minutes later after giving me more details about the ownership meeting I didn't need to know. I had to admit, though, John knew his stuff when it came to the business. He didn't pretend he couldn't be hit by a bus tomorrow. He had his family's future mapped out. My future was a blank canvas, now more than ever.

The only good thing about yesterday's phone call? Neither John nor Lauren so much as looked at me, or at each other. We were this triangle of avoidance. I should have let her take the phone from me and let him have it. I'd gone over every bit of that conversation in my mind, wishing I could have ended it before John revealed just how little he planned to stay out of things.

Yes, Boyce had been a disaster. John loved the guy. Boyce had been a truck whisperer, honest to a fault, humble, patient, friendly, the perfect employee. Basically, the only guy I knew worthy of Lauren, the only one I hadn't made fun of.

In that case, I hadn't needed to. Lauren had been young, barely twenty, and I think she got a little scared of how much Boyce liked her. Maybe he told her he loved her. Maybe he even asked her to marry him. Those were my own theories. All anyone knew was that Lauren ended things. Broke his heart. And he quit the next day. No two-weeks' notice. Nothing.

John mourned it all the more because Lauren didn't seem to care. She wasn't broken up over the guy at all, at least on the outside. Some of the guys at work had whispered 'heartless' behind her back after that. John saw it as immaturity on her part, a lack of emotional depth. But looking back, I think she just got careful about who she let really see her.

I wanted to take back all the stupid things I'd ever said about her boyfriends. The more I thought about it, the more I realized Lauren was as buttoned-up as I was. There was a whole world behind the mask she wore, and I wanted to see it. I wanted to understand her motives. Maybe even let her see mine.

But we couldn't even be friends.

CHAPTER 16

LAUREN

I drove to Melissa and Connor's house immediately after work. It was one thing for my dad to have conversations with Clay behind my back, but my sister-in-law? No. It wasn't happening.

Melissa answered the door with a crying Jax in her arms and Raelyn hanging on her leg. She looked ready to sell her kids to the circus.

"Lauren!" Raelyn released her mom's leg and dragged me inside. The house smelled like burnt popcorn and despair. I bent down to give her dogs a scratch. Sarge looked up at me with his large soulful eyes. His black fur was mostly gray these days. Poor baby. Buster turned circles, so excited to have someone new to sniff.

"Bad day?" I asked, looking over my shoulder at Melissa.

"Uh, you could say that. Raelyn dumped my hair serum all over the bathroom counter and tried to wipe it up with toilet paper. Besides being outrageously expensive, it's on backorder and my hair won't behave without it. I know that sounds ridiculous."

It would have sounded ridiculous if I hadn't noticed Melissa was having an extremely bad hair day. I'd always envied her corkscrew curls, but I wasn't aware of the effort behind getting them to look that way.

"Jax is running a fever, and he's so cranky. The doctor thinks it's just teething. He wouldn't nap today, not even in the car. Oh, and he blew out his diaper on the way home from the doctor so I think the teething theory is complete bunk. You should leave now while you can."

I took Jax from her arms in answer, even though it only made him cry harder. It didn't help when Raelynn chose that moment to dump out an entire bucket of Duplo Legos on the hardwood floor. Both Jax and I startled, only I didn't begin to wail.

"Come on, little guy. I know you love me." I rocked him gently while I walked around, dodging Legos and stopping occasionally to let him look at family pictures on the wall. Melissa had their whole lives chronicled in perfect square canvases. "Where's Connor?"

"He's bringing dinner. You want to stay and eat with us?"

In all the chaos, I'd forgotten why I was there. "You don't have to feed me. I just wanted to talk to you about something."

"Sure."

Jax's crying had turned into half-hearted gurgling. I looked down and saw he was soothing himself with half his fist in his mouth.

"Did my dad talk to you about potential guys I could date after I left last night?"

Melissa nodded, not looking the least bit repentant about it. "He felt so bad about Denver, and he asked me if I knew of any guys I could set you up with."

"Melissa, that was the whole reason I confronted him. I don't want my dad playing chess with my love life."

"You don't even want him interested in it?"

"No."

She frowned. "He loves you so much, Lauren. And I get it because I see the way Connor worries over Raelyn. He'd do anything for her. Dads just want to fix everything. They can't help themselves."

"Melissa, my dad called Clay and asked him to weasel into a

double date with whoever this guy is you want to set me up with. So he can spy on our date. Does that sound like he's sorry and wants to do better?"

Melissa stopped picking up stray socks and wrappers from the living room floor and turned to stare at me. "Clay told you this?"

I looked down at Jax and smoothed a wisp of hair over his forehead. "Yeah. Clay hates being put in the middle, and no wonder. I got pretty mad at him. It's the whole kill the messenger thing. And when my dad finds out Clay told me, he'll be mad at Clay, too." I hadn't felt sorry for Clay until the words left my mouth, and now I felt bad for ditching him at the middle school. He picked the wrong family to hang out with for life. We were drama queens. All of us.

"Poor Clay." Melissa looked thoughtful. "He won't let me set him up with anyone either."

"You've tried to set Clay up on dates?"

"Yeah. He wouldn't have it. Parker either. The whole unromantic bunch of you are driving me crazy. All I want to do is rearrange all the single people I know like Barbies and Kens, and none of you will let me."

I laughed, startling Jax. He didn't settle down again until I rocked him back and forth while wandering around the room.

"What do you want me to do?" Melissa asked. "Do you want me to talk to John?"

"No. Absolutely not. In fact, go ahead and give this guy my number. I'll go out with him. I might even talk Clay into going with us."

"Oh, Lauren. What sort of evil plan are you concocting?"

"Who says it's an evil plan?"

"You're a Harwood."

"Technically, so are you, sister. Besides, I have no plan." I really didn't. I just had a lot of curiosity about Clay on a date and a feeling my dad needed to learn just how murky the dating waters were these days. He thought he could pick a better guy than me? Let him try.

Melissa bit her nail. "This guy I want to set you up with, he's a real go-getter. If I tell him you're interested, don't be surprised if he calls right away. He doesn't believe in dawdling."

"And how do you know him?" I asked.

"He's my brother's ex-girlfriend's roommate's brother."

"Seriously?"

"I swear he's totally been vetted."

"Of course. This church-going, non-partier who's been too studious to date."

Melissa's eyes narrowed. "How do you know all that?"

Oops. "Um, well, Clay told me."

"Sounds like there's little he didn't tell you. And little John didn't tell him." I thought she'd be more suspicious, but she just muttered something about the way we Harwoods could talk the ear off a cornstalk and went back to putting her house in order while her hands were free.

I did stay for dinner, but left right after helping bathe the kids. Melissa and Connor needed time to themselves whenever they could get it. As it was, I caught them sharing secret looks as they raced to put the kids to bed. Bedroom eyes. Anticipation. I absolutely did not need or want them to have to spell out why it was time for me to go.

Jenny was still at a baby shower for her cousin, so I turned on the TV when I got home and flipped through the channels while I painted my nails, needing the noise but not really interested in watching anything.

When my phone rang with a strange number, I thought of what Melissa had said, but there was no way she'd already called the guy and he'd be calling me.

"Lauren Harwood?"

"That's me." Salesman for sure. He had ten seconds before I hung up on him, and only because it was an actual person and not some dumb recording.

"This is Noble Tuttle. Your sister-in-law told me to call you and set up a blind date. Is that still something you'd like to do?" He was so matter-of-fact about it. So business-like. So not my type. But maybe I was being a little harsh since I'd already planned on not liking him.

"Um, sure."

"I was thinking we could meet for dinner. I know a great Italian restaurant that's not too loud. Melissa said you were interested in this being a double date and you knew a couple you could ask. Would this Friday work?"

"It should. I'll ask them. Can I get back to you tomorrow?"

"Yes. What time should I expect your call?"

Expect my call? "How about seven?"

"Seven p.m.?"

"Yes." I would not be calling him first thing in the morning.

"Seven p.m. is fine. Good night."

"Good night." I hung up and laughed. I'd found the one for me. Noble Tuttle. The highly efficient, non-flirtatious man who scheduled a planning meeting to discuss our date. I guess I should get cracking on the double part of it, which meant texting Clay. I went to the kitchen and got a glass of ice water first because there was no reason to be so eager about texting Clay. Okay, I was a little eager. But only because there would be nothing businesslike or polite about our conversation. And that filled me with a strange joy I couldn't explain.

Lauren: You are going to make my dad so happy.

Clay: Spill it, Harwood.

Lauren: We're going on a double date. Which means get a date for Friday.

Clay: You need another favor? I'm sorry. Your tab is full. I expect payment first.

Lauren: This is my dad's favor, spy boy. Remember? He needs a thumbs up or thumbs down.

Clay: Are you sure about this?

Lauren: I'm living my #bestlife. Join me in blind date awkwardness.

Clay: Payment, Harwood. I accept cookies.

Lauren: So you keep saying. You must have a lot of faith in my baking skills.

Clay: True. I should monitor you. Come over tomorrow night at seven and make them in my kitchen.

Demanding little buzzard. Who did he think he was?

Lauren: I'm busy then.

Clay: Doing what?

Lauren: None of your business. I'll drop off Oreos in an untampered package. Take it or leave it.

Clay: Unacceptable. Your presence is required.

Whatever. He could have my silence as a counter-offer. I went back to flipping through the channels, occasionally checking in with Jenny. The baby shower had not been well attended, and therefore, Jenny was robbed of the chance to drop off a gift and sneak out like she'd planned. She was currently being forced to play games such as sucking juice out of a baby bottle in a chug-off and identifying baby food flavors spread across diapers to look like baby poo. Basically, an introvert's worst nightmare.

CHAPTER 17

CLAY

Parker and Evan had already written me off as a lost cause. The gamer rocking chairs Evan had in his living room were super comfortable, the perfect place to read on my phone and swap texts with Lauren. Maybe I would have liked video games more growing up if Parker hadn't been so competitive. He didn't sulk when he lost anymore, but I'd given up on winning against him years ago. At least when it came to the virtual game of football. In a real game, all bets were off.

It had been a while since I'd played on a PlayStation, and I kept mixing up what the triangle button did as opposed to the square or circle button. But I seriously wasn't interested in another tutorial along with ribbing about how I could fix a truck but couldn't handle a game controller.

"Who do you keep texting?" Evan asked.

"Oh, I have to find a date for Friday." It was better to bring it up now. I had no doubt both of them would find out about my double date with Lauren one way or another. Melissa and Connor weren't exactly known for keeping their mouths shut. Plus, I might need some help finding a date if Melissa didn't come through.

"Why Friday?" Parker asked. He weaved and bobbed with his player on the screen, his eyes never leaving it.

"Melissa talked Lauren into going on a blind date and she thought it would be less awkward if I was there with a date too."

"How is that less awkward?" Parker scoffed. "You two hate each other."

"Do you want to bring a date and go instead of me?" I asked.

"Nope."

"My girlfriend and I could go along with them," Evan offered.

I had not thought of that. And I needed a reason that couldn't happen. Stat.

"Melissa thought it would be better if it was blind dates for both of us. You know how it is if one couple is all over each other and the other has to sit there and watch."

I hadn't met Evan's girlfriend, so I didn't know if I was on target or not, but he shrugged, looking mollified. "True. My girl is not shy with affection. She says her love language is touch and mine is words of affirmation. She made me read this book—"

Parker elbowed him before he could continue. "Shut up and play, Evan. No one wants to hear about your love languages."

"Right, right." Evan was quiet for about three seconds before asking, "Who are you gonna bring, Clay?"

Didn't know, didn't care. Lauren was talking to me. Wanted me along. That was the important part. But I probably needed to call Melissa, considering I kept throwing her name into this. Three months ago, she offered to set me up with a friend and I told her never. With any luck, never was about to turn into just this once. "I'm letting Melissa set me up with someone."

Parker laughed. "One of the perks of being the black sheep in the family—I don't get roped into stuff I don't want to do. Have fun with that."

Oh, I planned to. "I'm gonna head out, guys. It's been real."

They swatted me off like a fly, not even trying to beg me to stay. Once I was in my truck, I called up Melissa, who sounded way too happy to hear from me, even at ten p.m.

"Clay, what's up with you?"

"Not much. It looks like I need a date for this Friday night."

"Well, okay then. I'll see what I can do. Is this for a double date, perhaps?"

"Yeah. With Lauren. Who is she going out with?"

"His name is Noble."

"Do you actually know him or is he like a friend of a friend of a friend?"

"The second one."

"And my date?"

She laughed. "Yeah, the second one. The girl I wanted to set you up with last time is dating someone else now, so I'll have to dig deeper."

"Beggars can't be choosers," Connor added from the background. Melissa laughed and said goodbye before hanging up on me.

I guess it was a good thing I didn't care who my date was.

Once I was home, I turned on my exercise app, which had been not so tactfully reminding me of the eight days since I last did their workout. At first, the little passive aggressive messages were funny.

Your abs will thank you....

You're never too busy for your health...

It's been six days since your last workout, but who's counting? Oh, we are...

Giving up already?

And there was no way to turn off the notifications. I knew because countless others had already Googled the same question.

Deleting the app would be admitting defeat, and I wasn't ready to do that. The app would know. The creators would be laughing. They were totally in my head. Jerks.

I did my three rounds of sit ups, pushups, lunges, squats, and high knees until the app gods were appeased.

After a shower, I checked my phone. Lauren still hadn't answered me, so I texted her one last time before going to bed.

Clay: Cookies…

CHAPTER 18

LAUREN

Another Tuesday morning meeting had me squeezed in between Herbert and Evan at the conference table. After yesterday's first ownership meeting, I had a better idea of what my dad meant by ownership. He basically wanted to make sure that if he died, the company would continue on without him. Until then, Parker and I were regular employees who happened to own shares.

I was secretly relieved. Parker was livid. But then, when wasn't he?

John looked around the table at all of us. "I'll be at the trade show in Las Vegas this weekend, and I plan to come home with at least two new mini excavators and possibly a new skid steer. But that means we need some equipment sold this week to offset costs. I asked Lauren to look over what's not renting. Give us your past sixty-day, six-month, and year-long losers in the different categories."

With all eyes on me, I pulled up my spreadsheets and went over what I thought needed to go and why. It was important to keep our fleet up to date, especially when we could use the new purchases to offset our tax liability at the end of the fiscal year.

What I didn't include in my presentation was the other numbers I'd run. I tracked who bought what and when. Five of the six sell-off suggestions had been purchased by Parker. In my opinion, he needed to be pulled from acquisitions and put solely on fleet management. Which probably meant swapping roles with Clay.

I was not looking forward to picking that fight. To Parker, spending company money was prestigious, a status symbol of his importance. Clay just wanted to fix stuff and stay out of the way. Which was exactly why they needed to switch. Clay was living below his abilities, and Parker wasn't focusing on his strengths.

How I wished the company was just a chessboard and I could move pieces around at will. Guys could say whatever they wanted about being the tougher sex. They were way more touchy feely when it came to their egos.

That was why I planned to start with the guy with the smallest ego, which funny enough, was Clay. He was all bark and no bite. Plus, I'd be armed with cookies. Or, at least, I would after I made them. I texted him after the meeting, watching from my desk while he pulled his phone out and looked at it.

Lauren: Fine. Tonight. Seven-ish p.m. Chocolate chip cookies. Provide ingredients and the recipe, or else.

Clay: Or else what?

Lauren: Or else you don't get cookies.

Clay: As you wish.

He turned and gave me a smolder Princess Buttercup would have swooned under. But not me. No swooning here. I stared him down before turning to my computer, focusing on looking bored and unconcerned. Whatever. Clay just liked to mess with me. Just like I liked to mess with him. We were… messy. I wasn't sure when my feelings for him had morphed from Parker's annoying friend into a complicated person I wanted to get to know on my own, but a part of me wished I could go back to ignoring him. Real ignoring, not this denial of how aware I was of him at all times.

How had Jenny put it? I sat up a little taller around him. I felt more. I wished she wasn't right.

I put my phone away so I wouldn't be tempted to check it. No more texting Clay at work. Someone was bound to catch on, the way gossip and rumors flew around here.

Dad wanted another ownership meeting with Parker and I right before I planned to leave for the day. I sighed, knowing this wouldn't be quick. I'd have even less downtime before I was supposed to call Noble.

I met up with Parker just outside of Dad's office.

"Do you know what this is about?" Parker asked.

"Your guess is as good as mine."

"Get in here, you two." Dad waved us in before turning to our tax guy, Barry, who was sitting in the corner looking like he was trying not to take up space. He glanced at the two of us before shuffling the papers in his lap nervously. He was a timid guy in general, but I had a bad feeling about what I was about to hear.

Dad motioned for Parker to shut the door behind him, and then rubbed his hands together. "Let's get right into it. Barry's here to help us with the paperwork. The long and short of it is, after meeting with him today, we think it's best if we get the ball rolling on this while the two of you are single. If either of you were to marry and get shares of the business after the fact, your spouse would be entitled to half in the case of divorce. It's a lot harder to take something that became yours before the marriage. And I hate to be crass about this, but it does happen." He looked to Barry to confirm what he was saying.

Barry gave us a nod. "This is true. We also plan to put in a clause that in the case of your death your spouse would get a payout from the company in return for cutting all ties to the business. The shares would revert to the other owners and not the living spouse. There would be no unexpected ownership transfer."

Parker leaned forward. "So you're saying, you'd take care of my wife and kids financially, but you'd take back the company's shares?"

"Exactly."

I frowned. Nothing they were saying was wrong; clinical maybe, but not wrong. But all I could think about was Clay being left out. We were signing paperwork today? If there was ever a time to say something, it was now. As fast as we were moving on this, it would soon be too late for regrets.

"What about Clay?" I asked.

Dad's eyebrows furrowed. "What about him?"

Parker hitched up his pants and turned to look at me. "Yeah, what about him?"

"Did you ever consider making him an owner? He's sort of like another kid, and he's just as invested in the business as the rest of us." Something I'd been so sure about managed to make me feel unsure the second it left my mouth. Especially based on the expressions from the other three in the room. Had I been wrong in thinking he should be included?

"You didn't say as much to him, did you?" Dad asked, staring me down.

"No." It came out automatically, and the panic hit me all at once. Because I was lying. I was lying to the two people who knew when I lied. I'd never been good at it.

"She did." Parker ran his hands through his hair. "She totally did. I can tell."

"Well, why not him?" I asked, trying to get back to the point. "It's just, this is moving really fast considering you told us yesterday to be patient—that it was a process that would take years. I thought there'd be a better time to discuss this, but I guess it's now."

Dad sat back down and looked at Barry. "To be honest, it hadn't occurred to me to include Clay."

"You're considering this?" Parker asked, looking from Dad to me and back again. "If I was the one who brought it up, you would've turned it down flat. But because Lauren says it, why not?"

I refrained from rolling my eyes. "This isn't about us, Parker. And why didn't it occur to you? Clay's your best friend."

Parker threw his hands up. "So this is about being better than me. Great. You win."

"That's not it at all." I didn't want to do this. It was like we were proving, right here and now, why we weren't mature enough for this. Squabbling coworkers were one thing. Squabbling owners were a disaster.

I turned back to Dad. "I'm not getting engaged tomorrow. Neither is Parker. Can we reschedule this for next week, or next month, and have some time to think about it? Because right now I feel like rejecting ownership altogether, but you've always taught us that important decisions shouldn't be made while we're upset."

"Yes, we're done for today." Dad shooed us both away, but called us back before we made it to the door. "We didn't get a chance to discuss the last ownership issue, and I want you to think about it before we meet again, considering the disaster this meeting's turned out to be. Owners cannot date employees of this company. Not now or in the future." He was looking at Parker, but he wasn't fooling anyone. He meant me. Yeah, Parker had dated a receptionist once, but nobody put up a fuss when she quit a few weeks later. He had been lucky enough to date an employee who wasn't good at her job.

I stared my dad down. "Why do we have to make a rule about it? For the last time, I'm sorry Boyce quit."

"This isn't just about Boyce. I don't want anyone taking advantage of either of you. And I don't want a culture of drama around here any more than we already have. Just think about it."

I hated when he was as logical as he was controlling. "Fine. I'll think about it."

"Good. But there is one more thing. We do need to know if you talked to Clay about sharing ownership, Lauren."

My stomach clenched. Back to this. "No. It was just an idea I was throwing out." I left before I had to lie harder to cover up what I'd done. In my worry about losing my chance to say something, I'd forgotten Clay's fear that I would—that I would try to micromanage his career. I stumbled to my truck and got in, throwing my bag across the seat. Why hadn't I asked for more time first instead of immediately mentioning Clay? Now I was clinging to a hope that nobody would talk to him about it unless they planned to bring him into ownership. I had just gambled with Clay's future, and there wasn't a thing I could do to fix it. Clay was going to hate me, and for once, it would be justified.

I drove home at a snail's pace, my mind so caught up in the meeting I passed streets without remembering the drive at all. It was freaky and frustrating, and I drove like a grandma just to be on the safe side. I carefully pulled into my parking spot in the apartment complex and ran upstairs.

Jenny was sitting at the kitchen table eating grapes. I ran to her and hugged her from behind, which made her laugh until she turned and saw my face.

"What's the matter? You look like someone picked you last for kickball."

"Never happened. I'm a kickball champion."

She wrinkled her nose. "Good for you, blondie. But seriously, what's the matter?"

I plopped into the chair next to her and stole a grape from her bowl only to put it back, earning me a glare. I had very high grape standards. No squishiness whatsoever.

Jenny picked it up and examined it before tossing it into the garbage. "I don't know what this grape did to offend you, but I'm not eating your cast-offs."

"I'm really wishing today that I had a punch-the-clock kind of job. One where you go home and think your boss is the worst, and don't have to feel guilty about it because it's nothing personal. Like when you're a kid and you think your teacher lives at school. No life beyond what you see. That's how I want to see my boss."

"What did your dad do this time?"

"Tried to pass on his hopes and dreams. Apparently there are a lot of tax implications and rules associated with that."

"Ah, the ownership thing. What sort of rules does he want you to follow in exchange for the keys to the kingdom?"

"Promising to never date an employee of the company."

Jenny leaned forward and studied me. "And you want to date somebody there? Who?"

"I don't want to date anyone there. I just don't want to be told I can't."

"Not even Clay?"

"No, I don't want to date Clay."

"Except you're going over to his house tonight, right?" Jenny looked pleased with herself.

"He's forcing me to make him cookies. It's not a date. It's actually payment for agreeing to go on a date with someone else."

"A date with someone else, but with you," Jenny clarified. "A double date."

I stood up and paced around the kitchen. "I should just call the whole thing off, shouldn't I? I'll call Noble right now and tell him never mind."

Jenny tossed a grape at me, which bounced off my shirt and rolled across the kitchen floor. "Is it rude if I ask you to pick that up for me? I just wanted to get your attention." She laughed at my deadpan stare and jumped up to get it herself. "Lauren, if you're not ready for ownership, you don't have to do this. You're twenty-three, and you have your whole life ahead of you. Just say you're not ready."

"Except my dad wants to plan it all now before Parker or I get married and our future spouses have a say and money ruins everything."

"Man, your dad is such a downer. And I get it. The business means everything to him. But does it mean everything to you?"

"I used to think it did. Now, I'm not sure." I got out a frozen dinner and studied the instructions before popping it in the microwave. Jenny was right. I didn't have to have all the answers today. I didn't even have to know why I was going over to make cookies for a person I had no intention of dating. Sometimes, people just wanted to make cookies and eat them, without any ulterior motives.

CHAPTER 19

CLAY

My house was clean, but not so clean it was suspicious. Same with me. I'd showered but decided to forego cologne. I did my hair but left it a little messy. I was in comfortable clothes but not so much that I looked like a slob. It was the same stupid balancing act I'd been doing for years, but I couldn't be greedy now. Friendship was a good first step for us. Maybe a step towards disaster, but then, what wasn't when it came to Lauren? It was a relief when she rang the doorbell, and I ran out of time to stress over how tonight might go.

She had her hair up in a messy bun and a snarky T-shirt on that said *Hang On, Let Me Overthink This.*

Couldn't have said it better myself. She looked perfect. The exact sort of trouble I liked from head to toe, and it always amazed me that no amount of time could go by where I wouldn't feel a kick of excitement the moment our eyes met. She gave me a self-conscious smile before pulling it back into her usual look of indifference.

I glanced behind her to see where she parked, and she turned to follow my gaze before fixing me with a stare. "You're afraid someone's going to see my truck in your drive, aren't you? Well, I beat you to it. I parked down the street."

Neither of us said anything for several seconds. How did we talk about the need to be secret friends, for no one to find out that we liked hanging out together? Heck, we couldn't even admit to ourselves we both wanted to be here. I didn't give a rip about cookies. I wanted to see Lauren. But I'd still used cookies as an excuse, for both our sakes.

Lauren brushed past me and threw her bag on the couch before walking into the kitchen and inspecting my cookie-making setup. I had everything out—pans and mixing bowls, utensils, all the ingredients, and aprons.

I grinned when Lauren picked up the matching apron set and held them out. Under a big cookie-shaped heart were the words, *Kiss the Cook*. I'd come home with the set after a white elephant gift exchange. Lauren had been there, but I didn't know if she remembered. I was sort of hoping she didn't so I could freak her out.

Moving closer, I took one out of her hands and slipped it over my head. "I saw these at the store and thought they'd be perfect for tonight."

She laughed and pushed me away. "Whatever. I remember you getting stuck with these aprons at the work Christmas party two years ago, Clay."

"Does that mean we can wear them without any pesky assumptions?" I picked up the one she'd put back on the counter and held it out.

Lauren crossed her arms. "I'm okay with a little flour getting on me. And don't worry about pesky assumptions. There will be no kissing of cooks going on. Don't worry."

"Are you sure you don't need one? I'm a messy baker. At least, I plan to be. I haven't really baked anything before."

"You plan to be messy?" She took the apron out of my hands and put it on, reaching back to tie it around her waist. She was about to say something, but her phone rang and she ran to get it from her bag. When she saw who it was, she put a warning finger to her lips before answering.

"Hi, Noble."

The dude talked for almost a minute before Lauren cut in with, "No, it's fine. I understand. Thank you for calling me back. Yes. Everything is set for Friday." She glanced up at me for confirmation, and I gave her a nod. "Is it okay if we meet at the restaurant?" There was a pause before she said, "Yes, I'm generally punctual."

He wanted to know if she was punctual? Who was this guy?

"Yes, separate tabs is fine."

I took a step towards her, but Lauren waved me off, putting a hand over her free ear as if she could block my opinion on the matter. My thoughts about Noble so far weren't nice ones, and she knew it.

"Okay, see you Friday." She dropped her phone back in her bag and looked up at me. "Now you can say it."

"Say what? That Noble sounds like a real winner? I mean, his name is a virtue. And he's a big fan of punctuality, so he has that going for him."

Her shoulders dropped and she sank into the couch. "Go on. I know this is your favorite game."

"Did he really tell you he wanted separate tabs? Because I'm paying for my date, and he can look like a cheapo while I pay for your dinner too."

"Clay, you can't."

"Watch me."

A thrill ran through me when she got up and stalked over to me, grabbing the front of my *Kiss the Cook* apron in her fist.

"You'll have your own date on Friday, and I'll have mine. No shenanigans."

"I like shenanigans."

"I know you do. That's what I'm worried about."

My hands came up of their own accord and rested on her hips. If she didn't step away, I was going to kiss her. And then we'd never get cookies, because she'd run. I knew it as well as I knew my own name.

Lauren's eyes dropped to my chest, and she stepped away,

rubbing her arms like she was cold. "Let's get cracking on those cookies. They're not going to make themselves."

We put a counter between us and got to work opening and mixing things. I did whatever she asked, her silent servant until she relaxed enough to look me in the eyes again.

"You want music?" I asked, moving over to the iPod docking station I had on the counter.

She shrugged. "Sure."

With no restrictions put on me, I scrolled to my Seventies playlist, which no one could ever resist dancing to, especially me. Our shop class teacher used to make us listen to a lot of Abba and the Bee Gees, and it just stuck with me.

When *Stayin' Alive* came on, Lauren's eyes widened, and she covered her mouth to hide a smile. I pretended not to notice and sashayed my way over to the oven to pre-heat it.

"What are you doing?" She leaned over the counter, resting her head on her arms and watching me. "This is not you."

"How do you know what's me?"

"Is this like, some sneaky seduction technique to get under my skin?"

I smiled. "On your skin."

She touched her neck self-consciously. Her beautiful neck that was turning red along with her face.

"So, let me get this straight. You're afraid to dance with me because you think it's some seduction technique I've been saving to use on you? Are you saying it would work? I'm asking for purely scientific reasons."

She rubbed her forehead. "I don't know what to think."

"Well then, relax, and *don't* overthink this."

She stared at me for several seconds before adding the chocolate chips to the dough in the bowl. And then her head rocked back and forth, and before I knew it both of us had our arms in the air and we were shaking our hips like no one was watching. And no one was. This whole night was our little secret.

We sang along to *How Deep is Your Love* while spooning out

the dough, and I had the tray of cookies in hand to put in the oven when Lauren froze.

"Did you hear that?" she asked, glancing toward the entryway.

"Hear what?" I put the tray down and moved to the iPod, pausing the music just in time to hear the doorbell again. Thank goodness I'd locked the door, because I had a pretty good idea who might drop by unannounced.

I tilted my head toward the hallway, and she didn't need more encouragement than that to go hide before I jogged to the entryway. I'd never wished for a salesman I could slam the door on more in my life.

But no, it was Parker. He walked in without an invitation the second I opened the door and walked straight to the kitchen, taking in the cookies in progress. He glanced back at my Kiss the Cook apron and raised one eyebrow. "You definitely need a social life more than I do."

"I was actually in the middle of an important... thought. And you interrupted." Dang it. Why didn't I have anything going on that gave me a legitimate reason to kick him out of my house?

"Well, sorry to interrupt. I'll be quiet so you can finish your thoughts or whatever. Are you going to stick those in the oven? It's preheated."

He made himself comfortable at my kitchen table with his feet propped up on another chair, and I picked up the tray and shoved it in the oven with a little more force than necessary.

"I'm gonna go use the bathroom." I stalked down the hall, closing the bathroom door on the way before checking the guest bedroom and then mine for Lauren. Where was she? I moved over to my closet and began sliding the door open. There was a tug on my ankle, and I jumped forward and hit the closet door before grabbing the sides and regaining my balance. I was lucky I didn't take the door off its tracks.

"Lauren!" I hissed, dropping to the floor next to her. "What are you doing? Stop trying to wrestle with me all the time."

"Yeah, you wish. So, who's over stealing my cookies? Parker

or Evan?"

"Parker. And technically the cookies were for me, so he's stealing *my* cookies."

"Our cookies. Fight me on it."

"I know you'd like to." I gave a strand of her hair a soft tug, enjoying our banter too much. It was the last of it we'd get tonight, which was a shame. "I'm sorry you're hiding in here."

"It's just how things are," she whispered. "But you better go back. I have to get out of your house."

I glanced up at my bedroom window. It was the best bet. The path to the back door was across from my kitchen, and there was a good chance Parker would see her if we tried that way.

I got up and lifted the blinds and undid the top and bottom locks before pulling the window open as quietly as possible. Then there was the screen to remove. I didn't want to ruin the screen unless I had to, and that meant removing the little screws before popping it out of the frame. This was taking too long.

"Hey, Clay," Parker hollered. "You didn't set a timer on the oven. How long do these cookies need?"

From the sounds of it, Parker was talking to the bathroom door. The one I wasn't in.

Lauren tapped my arm, mouthing, "go."

She'd have to make her own escape. I came out of my room and went out to set a timer for the cookies, giving it my best guess. Now that Lauren wouldn't get to eat them, I didn't care whether they were under or overdone.

Ten minutes later, my phone buzzed with a text. I checked it while Parker was too busy stuffing his face with piping hot chocolate chips cookies to notice. I wanted to punch him.

Lauren: Don't forget to put your screen back on and lock your window when you get a chance. You owe me cookies.

Clay: Next time at your place.

I put my phone away and placed a few cookies on a plate before sitting on the couch and turning on the TV.

"We should watch that documentary on drug traffickers," Parker suggested.

I didn't have a preference so I tossed him the remote before going in the kitchen to get a glass of milk. I took a detour to my bedroom first to lock my window. Lauren had propped the screen up against the house after removing it. I'd put it back on later.

"We had a really unproductive ownership meeting this afternoon," Parker said when I returned with my glass of milk.

"Oh yeah?" I stared at the TV, expecting him to continue, but when he didn't, I turned to look at him. He was staring at me thoughtfully.

"Does it make you uncomfortable for me to talk about it?" he asked.

"Talk about what?"

"Ownership."

"Why would it?"

"I don't know. I guess because you're sort of one of us, but sort of not."

There was no good way to answer that, so I didn't.

"Have you thought of saying something to John? About ownership?"

Not this again. Somehow, it made me feel worse that both he and Lauren had considered it, but not John. I got it. I wasn't one of his kids. Moving on. "No. Let's pretend we didn't have this conversation."

"Yeah, okay." He hit play on the show and any further conversation we had was about government corruption, and what it would be like to be a cop in a country where anyone could be bought.

Parker left soon after the show was over, and I got ready for bed, debating whether to call Lauren or not. I finally did while sitting in bed waiting for sleep to overtake me.

"Clay?"

"That would be me."

"Did the cookie monster ever leave?" she asked.

"Yes. I promise I'll make you new ones."

"I was only teasing. They were your cookies, Clay."

"Yeah, but I wanted to share them with you."

She was quiet for a minute. Likely not used to hearing anything sweet coming out of my mouth.

"What did Parker want?"

"I don't know. To watch TV somewhere else. To make uncomfortable conversation."

"What do you mean uncomfortable?"

I paused, not sure how honest I wanted to be. But being real with Lauren was this new refreshing thing I was getting addicted to. I wanted her to see me. The real me. "Parker asked how I felt about the company ownership."

Lauren sucked in a breath. "What do you mean?"

"I mean, he asked if I thought about saying something to John. And the answer is still no, by the way."

I thought she'd launch into me, but Lauren was quiet. Eerily, guiltily quiet. And I refreshed that conversation I'd had with Parker with new eyes based on her reaction.

"Lauren, did you say something to him? Oh, no. Did you say something at the ownership meeting today?"

"I'm sorry. It's just, John moved up the timeline. Like he wanted us to sign papers and everything right then, and I thought if I didn't say something it would be too late, and I knew you never would."

I dropped the phone, stung. I knew she was sorry, sorry enough to admit it right away and not cover it up. But I was still angry. Everything I wanted was getting twisted and tangled in ways that would end with me losing it all.

"Clay, say something."

I ignored her, but I didn't end the call either. I just breathed in and out, and thought. Finally, I picked back up the phone and put it to my ear. "Why, Lauren? Now it's going to nag at John. It will be in the back of his mind when he talks to me, and it's going to annoy him. But he's not going to change his mind. He's a decisive guy. Don't you think he's thought this through?"

"I wish I could take it back. I didn't think of the consequences if he didn't agree with me, and I'm sorry for that. I don't think John's going to be annoyed, though. You're part of us."

"I'm not. I have to go." I hung up and launched back against my pillow. Everything was wrong. The anxiety of going into work the next day kept me up for the next few hours. I even tried Lauren's technique of reading paperbacks. I had a biography of John Adams on a shelf and got two chapters in before I threw it on the floor and attempted counting sheep.

CHAPTER 20

LAUREN

The rest of the work week had me on pins and needles, but Dad was leaving for the convention in Las Vegas, and that's where his focus was. He didn't talk to me or Parker about ownership issues, and as far as I could tell, he didn't talk to Clay much either. We sold off several key pieces of equipment just in time, and I left work on Friday afternoon so ready for the weekend. I had a date to get ready for, and punctuality was key. Whatever Clay might say about it, I liked a guy who was straight-forward and asked for what he wanted. Clay just didn't like it because he didn't see the value in it.

Jenny was off visiting with a college friend who had flown in for the weekend, so I got ready by myself, keeping an eye on the clock. I decided to go with a floral sundress with ruffles on the straps and cute red buttons down the front. I wasn't much of a dress girl, and I hated that it was Clay I thought about when I looked in the mirror, hoping I looked okay.

After grabbing my cute matching purse and checking its contents, I locked up and drove to the restaurant where we were meeting, following the GPS directions. I pulled into a parking spot ten minutes early, and peering around, spotted

Clay's truck in the row behind me. He was early, too.

I stayed in my truck with the air conditioning blowing over me, not surprised when Clay tapped on the passenger window a minute later. I unlocked the door and he hopped in.

"Hey," I said. There was still that weird tension between us, left over from work and our last real conversation together.

"Hey, yourself. You look nice." He looked me over, and I appreciated his notice in a totally different way than I had when Denver used to smile at me like that. I felt Clay's gaze all the way to the center of me. His admiration was not for show. It was not an act. It was solely about me and for me, and it filled me up more than any pretty words could ever do.

"Who ended up as your date?" I asked, needing to break eye contact with him. I rested my arms on the steering wheel and watched a couple walk inside the restaurant.

"About that." Clay groaned. "You will owe me for this until the end of time. Parker laughed when I told him. Like, leaned over holding his stomach, and just about died, he was so tickled. It turns out Melissa's friend of a friend of a friend is Denise Perkins. Do you remember her? My grade in high school?"

"No. What's wrong with her?" I felt suddenly protective of this unwanted date of his.

"She was slightly obsessed with me back in the day."

"Relax. I'm sure she barely remembers you now."

Clay huffed out a laugh. "Of course you'd say that. It's impossible for you to imagine anyone would ever find me worth remembering. So, where's your date? Mr. Punctual?"

I glanced at the clock. "He's still got four minutes." To some people, being punctual meant neither early nor late. I had a feeling Noble would show up right on time.

Clay scooted closer, and I gave him the side eye. With a bench seat and no console in the middle, my truck was perfect for getting nice and cozy, but now was not the time or place, and we were definitely not the right people. I was not imagining otherwise. Okay, I was banishing that thought immediately. Well, I was working on banishing it.

I put my palms down on the seat between us before he could move in closer and glared at him. "What are you doing?"

"We should have code words for when this date goes south." He whispered it like we were spies and the truck might be bugged.

"*If* this date goes south," I corrected.

"Semantics." Clay placed his palms over mine, sending all sorts of signals to my brain. I liked the way it felt, but he couldn't know that. Ever. We'd become the combative friends we were always meant to be. Anything more was a dangerous fantasy on my part.

I cleared my throat. "So, when I'm right and Denise barely remembers you, I'll say, 'She's just as beautiful as you said, Clay.'"

"And when Noble shows up late after he asked you to be punctual, I'll say, 'Time is money. Let's go in.'"

"What if we're both wrong?" I looked down at our hands, willing him to lift his first, because if I did, it would draw attention to the fact that I was affected by his touch.

"If you're wrong about Denise, I'll need a real code. Something that means 'help me.' So, when I say, 'I could really go for some artichoke dip,' you have to get us out of there. For reals, Lauren."

He was serious, and it made me want to laugh. He was totally terrified of his date. She must have been scary in high school, poor girl.

"Promise me."

"Fine, I promise. But then we're even forever and I don't owe you any more favors."

He lifted his hands and put up a pinkie. I linked mine with his. And we swore on emergency plans and never owing favors.

A knock sounded on the passenger window, startling us. It was Noble, right on time. Surprise, surprise. I'd described my truck to him, and he knew what I looked like because Melissa had shared a picture of me.

I jumped out the driver door and walked around to say hello.

Noble gave me the firmest handshake I'd ever received, and that was saying something, considering I worked with mechanics and construction guys.

Then he shook Clay's hand, and between the two of them, it was practically an arm wrestling match. Just what we needed here, an unspoken rivalry within three seconds of meeting each other.

"Where's your date?" Noble asked Clay, looking around.

"She should be here soon."

"Call her and let her know she can join us inside. I made a reservation, but I'd hate for them to give our table away." Noble gestured for me to go ahead of him, then fell in step beside me towards the entrance. He was holding a buzzer from the restaurant, so I wasn't sure what his concern was. Obviously, he'd already gone inside and informed them we were here.

"Time is money," Clay said cheerfully from behind us.

I glanced back and rolled my eyes at him. Clay had not pulled out his phone to call his date as Noble directed, and I doubted it was just because he didn't like taking orders from a bossy stranger. I had a feeling Clay didn't care whether his date showed up or not. He seemed perfectly happy to remain the third wheel, even making polite conversation with Noble while we all stood together in the foyer. Well, an outsider would consider the conversation polite. I knew what Clay was really doing—asking Noble open-ended questions in hopes he would further reveal his forceful personality. I wish I could say it wasn't working.

I tried to cut in when Noble took a breath between comments about his political volunteer work, but Noble actually put his pointer finger up in front of my face and continued on for another three minutes before waving out his hand as if giving me permission to proceed.

"What were you going to ask?" he prompted.

I shook my head. "I don't remember." The stupid buzzer in his hand was lifeless. What was the point of a reservation if we had to wait just as long as the rest of the people packed in here like sardines?

Noble said he picked the place because it wasn't loud, and if we were comparing it to a joint with peanuts on the floor and line-dancing waiters, that would be true.

A large group came through the double doors. Clay moved closer to us to make room for them, his chest brushing against mine and our fingers touching briefly before he moved sideways past me to the wall. Noble had done something similar minutes ago, and the effect it had on me was night-and-day different.

Chemistry was a funny thing. I truly believed you could create chemistry with a person if you both wanted it. You could choose love. You could build it. None of this falling out of love business. But I didn't particularly like Noble so far, and so had no desire to create anything with him except a lot of distance after this date.

And speaking of wanting to create distance, I knew the moment Denise Perkins walked in because Clay hunkered down against the wall until I was completely blocking him. It didn't matter. She ran straight for him and wrapped him in a hug.

"Clay, I can't even tell you how much fate had a hand in this. I've been thinking about tracking you down for years. And now here we are." Her large, liquid eyes sparkled with a fervor that probably would have scared me even without Clay's warnings.

When the length of their hug reached awkward territory, he managed to wriggle free from her and turned to introduce us.

Noble gave her one of his bone-crushing handshakes, and I gave her a little wave before immediately complimenting her on her blouse. It was the first thing that came to mind because the bright tangerine color would be burned on my retinas for days to come.

"Oh, this thing?" She looked down and smiled. "I actually ordered it off of Facebook. Those ads get me every time."

I'd ordered several hit-and-miss items off Facebook ads myself, so while we continued to wait, I kept the conversation going about that. Denise was fun to talk to, and I almost forgot why I thought she was weird until she gazed at Clay again and sighed. "You're so handsome. I want a picture of us together before we leave tonight. Why aren't you on social media? I couldn't find you anywhere."

Clay threaded his fingers together. "I don't know. I just don't like social media."

"Well, I don't want to lose touch again. Promise you'll call me after tonight."

Clay looked torn. I knew he didn't want to promise something he had no intention of doing, but the truth might hurt just as much.

Thankfully, the buzzer in Noble's hands started hopping, and that was enough of a distraction for Denise to let it go.

Following the hostess, Noble and I slid into one side of a booth, and Clay and Denise sat on the other. She cozied up next to him and wrapped her hand around his upper arm. "Muscles," she murmured, giggling to herself.

I picked up my menu and studied it, looking for something inexpensive, knowing the discussion over the bill would be less awkward the less I spent.

"What's good here?" I asked Noble.

"Everything. I especially enjoy the clams Italiano and the prawns alla busara."

"Mmm." I was not adventurous when it came to seafood. Maybe it was because I'd been landlocked my whole life, but I wasn't about to dip my toe in tonight. I'd stick with the Italian staples I was familiar with.

I asked for water when the waitress came to take our drink orders and avoided the knowing look Clay threw my way when everyone else got fountain drinks.

Noble ordered a calamari appetizer for us, and then instructed the waitress to split the check into four equal parts. She nodded and left before the rest of us could react, probably eager to get to her other tables.

Denise looked confused, "Wait, should I...?"

Clay touched her hand. "I'm paying for your dinner. I don't know what he's talking about."

Denise melted into him. "Thank you. It would be okay if you didn't, I just wasn't expecting—"

"Lauren and I talked about it beforehand," Noble cut in. "We had planned to split the bill. I thought you would have told them that, Lauren. I thought that's what we agreed on."

I opened my menu again, taking a deep breath. He was berating me? Seriously? And why did we have to have this discussion at the beginning of dinner and not at the end? My stomach was in knots as it was. If it was just the two of us, Noble and I, this would be the part where I faked an emergency and left, but that wasn't an option with others involved.

"Lauren told me," Clay said, an edge to his voice. "I just didn't agree with it. Sometimes we have to compromise on things."

Noble gave a curt nod. "Okay, that's fair. I'm sorry. What's everyone ordering?"

"The cheese ravioli," I said, closing my menu.

"Not the clams italiano or the prawns alla busara?" Noble seemed offended that I'd ignored his suggestions.

"I think I'll have the ravioli, too," Clay announced.

"Me, too." Denise smiled at me. I wasn't sure if it was a show of solidarity on her part or an attempt to not be left out, but either way, somehow this had become the three of us against my date.

The next hour was the longest ever. Noble sulked while he ate his seafood, Clay played an unsuccessful game of "try to keep Denise's hands off of me," and I doodled on the white paper table covering with a pen from my purse while nibbling on bites of ravioli. Clay excused himself at one point, and I knew he went and paid for all of us because I watched to make sure he wasn't escaping and leaving me there.

His eyes met mine when he returned, and they held a question. When? When could we get out of there? That's what both of us were thinking. Denise was almost finished, and the two of us watched and waited. Noble didn't seem to be in any hurry either. If I left Clay with Denise and Noble, he'd never let me live it down, and I felt the same way about him leaving me. We were stuck in this stupid restaurant standoff.

"Well, this has been a lovely night. Is everyone ready?" Clay finally asked. He put his napkin down. "Denise, let me walk you to your car."

"What about the bill?" Noble asked, peering over my head for the waitress.

"I took care of it," Clay said. "You ladies ready?"

I nodded. "Thank you for the date, Noble. Nice to meet you." I took the arm Clay offered and walked off, not caring what Noble's reaction was. Denise, on Clay's other arm, shivered like an excited puppy. She leaned toward me. "Oh, you poor thing, Lauren. I wish there were two Clays. He's just the perfect date."

I could feel Clay's tension through his shirt. How was he supposed to shut down such sweetness, however misguided?

"You two have a good night," I said, once outside. I let go of Clay's arm and walked towards my truck. He could wriggle out of her goodnight kiss on his own.

"Lauren Harwood, you come back here right now."

I stopped and looked back at him. His face held enough shock that I was pretty sure he didn't know where he was going with his outburst yet. Panic. He was running on pure panic. This ought to be good.

"You don't have to hide your disappointment in your date tonight. I saw the tears you were holding in. Let it out, girl."

He held out his free arm.

Denise, on his other side, looked concerned. "I think she's okay."

"Nope. I know Lauren. She holds these things in until they give her cramps. Debilitating cramps. I should drive her truck home just to make sure. She eats artichoke dip when she gets sad, and then turns into a bad friend who doesn't keep her promises."

"Um, okay." Denise pulled her keys out of her purse. "I'm sorry about the cramps, Lauren. Call me later, Clay."

He nodded. "I will."

After Denise got in her car and drove off, I came back over and socked him lightly in the stomach. "Why'd you tell her you'd call her? That's mean."

"I will call. And I'll tell her I'm in a relationship with someone else."

"No, you're not."

"I'm in a friendship relationship with you. It's an exclusive friendship relationship."

"Whatever. Cramps?"

"You gave me no choice." He glanced behind us and motioned for me to follow him. "Noble's coming out," he mouthed.

Yeah, I did not want to have a second farewell with that guy, so I ducked behind the Suburban next to us with Clay until Noble got into his car and drove off.

CHAPTER 21

CLAY

That had been a lot of work for one of the worst dates of my life. Part of me wanted to go home, take two aspirin, and throw myself into bed. But the other part wanted redemption. I wanted the night I was supposed to have.

I walked Lauren to her truck. "I'll follow you home."

"Why?"

I shrugged. "I don't know. So I can walk you to your door. Make sure you get in okay."

"Invite yourself in," she added.

I clutched my chest. "Lauren, I would never. What kind of guy do you think I am? Besides, your roommate will be there, right?"

Lauren rolled her eyes. "I didn't mean, invite yourself in like that. You wish. I just meant, you'd invite yourself inside to hang out and talk me into staying up late to watch a movie."

"I accept."

She shook her head at me and got into her truck. I took that as a yes and followed her home, parking my truck in the guest spot across from her.

We walked together up the steps to her apartment, and she unlocked her door and glanced back at me. "Come in. Don't be a nuisance."

"I feel welcome already."

"I'm sure you do." She went into her bedroom and came out a few minutes later wearing soft pink pajama pants and a gray T-shirt. "Jenny's still out with her friend from out of town. She says she'll be home at eleven-thirty."

"Do you want me to go?" All joking aside, I wanted her to want me there, not push myself into her life. At some point, our teasing had to be backed by something real.

Lauren studied me before plopping down on the couch and holding out the remote.

I took it carefully, waiting for her to pull it back at the last second, but she didn't. "Who are you, and what have you done with Lauren?"

"I'm too tired to pick." She rested her head back. "I hate when Jenny's not here."

"Is she gone a lot?"

"Hardly ever. She doesn't seem to mind when I'm gone, but I don't like being here alone without her."

"So I'm a space filler." I sat down next to her and turned on the TV.

"Basically. It's you or I start talking to my house plants." She turned her head and smiled at me. "You offered, you know."

"True." I found *Miss Congeniality* and left it there, knowing it was a movie she liked. I wasn't really paying attention to the screen so it didn't matter. Lauren had her legs curled up in the most uncomfortable position, and after watching her shift them to the floor and back up again, I reached out and draped them across me, wrapping my hand around her knee.

She stared at the screen as if she hadn't noticed at all, but I felt her tense and then slowly relax little by little, though she kept her arms folded—a clear message of *there will be no hand-holding*.

A few minutes later, she yawned and grabbed the remote,

pausing the TV. "I'm gonna get water. Do you want some?"

"I'm okay."

I missed the weight of her legs on me the second she left, and I wondered if she got up on purpose so she could put more distance between us. Sure enough, when she returned, she sat down on her end and hunched over, staring at the TV. It looked about as relaxing as a massage from the world record holder for longest fingernails.

I reached over and stole the glass of water out of her hands, finishing it off.

She gave me an indignant glare. "I asked if you wanted water."

"Well, now I do. You need more?"

She shook her head.

I got up to put the cup by the sink, sitting as far away from her as possible when I came back. "I'm so glad you decided to put some space between us. I was going to say something if you didn't."

She ignored me and watched the movie, absentmindedly rubbing her bare arms like she was cold.

"Do you need a blanket?" I asked.

"Shh."

Yeah, because William Shatner's singing was so riveting. I got up, walked straight to her bedroom, and pulled her comforter from the bed. It smelled like her hair, with that sexy bubble bath scent I hadn't stopped thinking about since I'd first noticed it.

"Are you sniffing my blanket?" She looked mortified. "Does it smell?"

I smiled. "It smells like you, and trust me, that's not a bad thing."

She reached out, expecting me to hand it to her, but I kept walking and sat on my end of the couch with it balled up in my lap. Then I sniffed it again, just to make her extra self-conscious.

She stared at me for several seconds before launching herself across the couch in a surprise attack. At least, she thought it would come as a surprise.

I was totally prepared for it and held on with all my might.

She growled and sat back, keeping hold of the small corner she'd extracted from me.

"I never said I wouldn't share." I let go and draped the comforter over both of us, tucking it into her sides before sitting back and letting her watch the movie in peace.

Well, for a few minutes anyway. Our hands on top of the blanket were too far apart for my taste. I moved mine closer to hers and left it there, close enough that she stared at my hand for several seconds before her eyes returned to the screen.

If I didn't see it with my own eyes, I would have called any other witness a liar. Slowly, slowly, slowly, her hand slid over and breached the final distance, until her pinkie finger reached out and caressed mine ever so softly.

Then her legs in her pink pajamas shifted over a bit until they were crossed with mine at the ankles, and the next thing I knew her face was turned towards me and she wasn't watching the movie anymore.

"Lauren," I whispered. "Are we friends?"

"Yes," she whispered back. Her heartbeat fluttered like a little bird's. I could see it pulsing on her neck.

"Are we more than friends?"

"I don't know." She paused the TV and dropped the remote on the blanket where it slid to the floor.

I laced my fingers with hers and stared into her earnest face. Should I kiss her? There was no going back to normal once I did. I knew it, but the full truth of it didn't hit me until her lips touched mine. I'm not sure who made the first move, maybe we both did.

All I knew, was that kissing Lauren was like liquid fire shooting through my veins.

I ran my hand through her hair and softly down her neck, angling my head so she wouldn't have to work so hard to reach me. Any moment, she was going to pull away, tell me this was a mistake, that kissing me was wrong. I forced myself to edge back several times, giving her that chance, but all she did was move closer, making a little noise of distress until I closed the distance again and met her demands. Her bottom lip was mine. Her top one too. I kissed the soft spot on her neck just below her jaw, and she angled her head up for me to reach. I was a goner.

It was the stupid chime of a text message on her phone that finally broke the spell. She backed away from me, her eyes wide and filled with wonder. Her lips were slightly swollen, and her skin had the most beautiful blush running from her forehead down to her neckline.

She shuddered. "Maybe we shouldn't have done that."

Just as I predicted. There were a lot of things I could've said to tease her about the hypocrisy of her words just then, but I had no desire to make her regret this any more than she already did.

She grabbed her phone from the arm of the couch and checked it. "Just my dad sending pictures of him standing with other construction nerds with lanyards around their necks."

"He does love the conventions." I didn't want to talk about her dad. Right now was about the two of us, Lauren and me.

A silence settled between us, and Lauren couldn't take it. Throwing off the blanket, she got up and walked the length of the room and back again. Her hair was adorably mussed. I guess I owned some of the blame for that.

A minute later, the lock clicked, saving Lauren from further overthinking. Jenny came in the door, dropping a shopping bag off to the side. She looked from me to Lauren, and her eyes widened slightly before she recovered. "How did the date go?"

"It was a disaster," Lauren said with a little laugh. She looked back at me as though with new eyes. "I'll walk you out, Clay."

I got up quickly, made sure I had my phone and keys, and stepped out onto the porch. Lauren closed the door behind us, her eyes on the ground. "I don't know what to say." Her regret and embarrassment was palpable, and I realized my fear of scaring her off by saying the wrong thing had led me to say nothing at all after kissing her. Thoroughly kissing her. But I couldn't let my focus go there. Right now was just as important.

"Can I see you tomorrow?" I asked, reaching out to run my hand down her arm to her wrist before picking up her hand.

"Do you think that's a good idea?"

"I think it's a great idea. I'll be here at seven."

"A.M.?"

"Yeah." I kissed her cheek and walked off, only glancing back once to make sure she went back inside her apartment.

CHAPTER 22

LAUREN

How would I rate kissing Clay Olsen? Five stars. Two enthusiastic thumbs up. Fireworks. Everywhere. He had wrecked me for all other men with one kiss, and I'd made sure he knew it the way I'd clung to him.

I gripped my hair as the embarrassment of it all washed over me again. One kiss wasn't exactly accurate. It had been a lot of kissing. Several times, he'd pulled away, and each time I'd reeled him back in, like I couldn't get enough, because... I couldn't.

What if this became just another blip in our weird history? That one time our flirting got out of hand and wasn't that so funny? He'd have a new reason to tease me, to keep his distance so my dad and Parker wouldn't find out we'd ever spent time together.

My comforter smelled like him even after a fitful night's sleep. Thanks to his pronouncement that he'd be here at seven, I'd set my alarm for six, but now it was six-fifteen and I couldn't get my body to cooperate and actually get out of bed. It was Saturday morning for crying out loud. I finally reached over and picked up my phone from the nightstand, sending him a text.

Lauren: I'm rescheduling this mysterious meeting we're having until ten. Because… reasons.

Clay: No need. I'll just come snuggle with you until you're ready to get out of bed.

Lauren: You will not.

Clay: <Grinning emoji> See you at 7.

I smiled in spite of myself. What was I supposed to do about Clay? I'd been there when my dad called him and talked about me not dating people in the company, and Clay didn't even know about the stupid clause I was supposed to sign to make it official. We could not date. He knew it. I knew it.

But was this dating? We didn't have to define it. No labels required. We were just two people who liked spending time together because it was forbidden. I groaned at my own stupidity and rolled out of bed. I needed a shower before Clay got here.

I passed Jenny's room and ducked my head in to talk to her, but she wasn't there. What the heck? I quickly texted her and was relieved when she responded right away.

Lauren: Where are you?

Jenny: It's a long story. Noah from work invited me to go on a hot air balloon ride this morning. His date bailed on him. The tickets are two hundred bucks!

Lauren: Awesome! I want details!

Jenny: I'll spill later. Gotta go.

It must have been really last minute. The two of us had stayed up way too late squealing and speculating about Clay, and there was no mention of hot air balloon rides.

Speaking of Clay, I'd better hurry. I ran back to my room for my shower comb and then locked myself in the bathroom for a long shower. Too long.

I was heading back to my room in my bathrobe when a

knock sounded at the door. Of course he'd be early, the stinker. Or maybe he was right on time. I tended to lose track of time when glorious hot water was raining down on my head.

I'd just text him and tell him to wait. I tiptoed back to the bathroom thinking I'd left my phone on the counter, but it wasn't there. Had I left it in Jenny's room? Her room was slightly below tornado level of messy and the thought of searching it had me sighing.

Surely Clay would text me something snarky by now and I'd hear the chime. I stood in the hallway listening.

The knock came again, and I rushed to the door and checked the peephole. Clay was waiting patiently with his arms loaded down with canvas bags. I wasn't even sure how he'd knocked. Maybe with his forehead?

I opened the door a crack and stuck my head out. "Hold on. I'm still getting ready. Wait a full minute so I can run back to my room. Then come in and wait in the living room."

"Sure thing." He grinned at me, and I couldn't help grinning back before shutting the door.

I took off like a woman on a mission, but my big toe caught on the edge of the carpeting, and with a little scream, I went sprawling, giving my knee a nasty rug burn and almost losing my robe.

"Are you okay?" The door cracked open.

"Close your eyes! Stay right there!"

I got up quickly and tied the robe back around myself before turning to make sure he was obeying, which he was. He stood frozen in the doorway with his eyes squeezed shut, half the bags now at his feet, and half in his arms. One bag had spilled over, revealing its contents—a roll of store-bought cookie dough and his kiss the cook aprons. What kind of adorableness had he planned for us today? I snuck a little closer and studied his face while he had his eyes shut tight. He was freshly shaven and smelled really nice. I almost kissed his perfect mouth before common sense took over, and I dashed back to my room and shut the door behind me.

My eyes zeroed in on my phone peeking out from under my covers like a little traitor.

Dressing as quickly as possible, I came out to find him in my kitchen, examining my house plants sunning themselves in the window above the sink. He turned and studied me, looking amused. "I've been trying to piece together what just happened. Did you fall?"

"Yes. I tripped."

"And why did I have to close my eyes?"

"Um, because I was… there was a wardrobe malfunction, okay?"

He laughed so hard I reached out and smacked his arm.

He smirked. "But while I had my eyes closed, you came up to me. What was that about?"

"I didn't come up to you." I turned away from him and peered in one of the canvas bags. He had a bocce ball set inside. That couldn't have been fun to hold for five minutes at my door.

"I could feel you breathing on me, Lauren."

"I was spying in your bags."

"You're a terrible liar."

"Okay, what did you think I was doing?" I crossed my arms, hoping to look mature and calm, and not like he was totally on to something.

"Well, I didn't find a 'kick me' sign on my back. And I checked for a marker mustache. Did you drop itch powder down my back that hasn't kicked in yet?"

"Hold on, I'm taking notes." I pulled my phone out of my back pocket and began typing in his suggestions. I was doing it as a joke. Mostly.

"Come on, Lauren."

I looked up from my phone. "Let me get this straight. You think I tripped in my bathrobe on purpose? All so I could prank you while your eyes were closed?"

"You were in your bathrobe?"

I pressed my palm into my forehead. "This conversation is officially over, dude. Now what are we doing in my kitchen?"

"Making omelets." After going through my lower cupboards, he found a frying pan and set it on the stove. "Unless you have other breakfast ideas. I'm okay with whatever you want to eat."

"You had me at omelets." I got out the salt and pepper for him and pulled the butter and milk out of the fridge. "What else do you need?"

He rummaged around in our fridge and pulled out various things I had never considered putting in eggs before and chopped them up small before mixing them into the bowl. I was preparing myself for the worst, but the final product was amazing. I almost licked my plate.

I looked up and caught him staring at me, and was suddenly self-conscious about my damp hair and lack of makeup. "I'm gonna go get ready for the day."

I retreated to my room and got to work blow drying my hair before putting in a little bit of curl. Then I started on my makeup.

Clay came in and sat on the edge of my bed, watching. He picked up my hairbrush and twirled it in his hands. "Are you ready to have a real conversation?"

I met his eyes in my mirror. "What do you mean?"

"I thought you might need some time to process after last night. I know I did."

He was being so serious, which was so unlike him. His serious face was even more handsome than his mischievous one.

"I like you, Lauren."

I bit my lip to hold back a smile. "I like you, too."

It felt too much like middle school, where even that little admission was enough to send both of us off to consult with our friends about what the next move was. Exchanging friendship bracelets perhaps? Sitting by each other on the bus?

"Are you laughing at me?" He reached out and lightly poked my side. "I like you. We can say that now, right?"

"Yeah, we can say it."

"Can I say I want to spend as much time with you as possible? Because I do."

I stopped putting on blush and flipped around to face him. "Why?" I wasn't even sure what kind of answer I was looking for. All I knew was that before this week I thought he hated me.

He leaned forward, putting his hands out like a plea. "I've spent a lot of time and energy, more than I want to admit, making sure nobody ever suspected I've had feelings for you. And I'm tired. I'm tired of pretending this isn't what I want. The biggest reason I felt like I had to hide it was because I figured you wouldn't... reciprocate."

He was afraid of rejection. Wow. My throat closed off and I didn't trust myself to speak, so I covered his hands with mine and traced the lines across his wrists with my thumbs.

"Say something," he whispered.

"Okay. I have a confession. A small one." I wasn't ready to reveal everything I was feeling, but I could give him this.

"I'm all ears."

I met his eyes, though I knew my face was growing hot. "I did sneak over to you at the door, but not to peek in the bags. I thought about kissing you and then chickened out. Or came to my senses. But we're not talking about the bathrobe thing again, okay?"

I'm sure whatever he'd been about to say in response would have been good, but Jenny chose that exact moment to come barging through the door to the apartment and stomping down the hall to my room. From the look on her face, either she was about to ugly cry or shout in anger.

"I hate Noah Edgeworth. I never want to see him again!" She burst into tears.

Ah, so it was both. "What happened?"

Clay moved out of her way and motioned that I should call him. A fist-sized ache started in my chest, but I ignored it and patted the spot on the bed he had just vacated. Jenny didn't act this way over nothing. A breakdown from her like this was rare.

Jenny collapsed into the spot next to me, laying back with her hair fanned out. "You don't have to go, Clay," she hollered. "Just pretend to watch TV or something for a few minutes."

There was a muffled, "okay," in response, and Jenny and I laughed, her through the tears streaming down her face, and me in relief. I didn't deserve such a good friend and roommate.

"What did Noah do?" I asked, reaching over to my desk and retrieving my tissue box. I handed it to her and waited while she blew her nose.

Jenny sniffed. "His date, the one who cancelled, called while I was standing there with him and asked if it was too late to come, and the hot air balloon pilot guy said he didn't care as long as she got there in the next ten minutes. So we waited for her. I should have left right then, but like an idiot, I went on a date with another girl competing for his attention, and she was playing to win, let me tell ya. She spent the entire time clinging to him, pretending she was scared. Okay, maybe not pretending. We were all scared. What was I thinking going up hundreds of feet in the air in a wicker basket? I was terrified and miserable, and he kept trying to make the situation better, and like a dude, he totally made it worse."

"I'm so sorry, Jen."

"Me too. And I woke up at the crack of dawn to get all ready and now I'm—" she let out a yawn that seemed to go on forever. "I'm so tired."

"Are you hungry? I could make you something."

She shook her head. "I'm going to climb back in bed and pretend I don't have to see him on Monday for carpool. Go be with your man."

"Are you sure?"

Jenny climbed off my bed and stretched. "Yes, I'm sure. But if you wanted to bring me back donuts I wouldn't complain."

"Done."

Jenny reached back and stole my fuzzy heart pillow she'd been laying her head on and escaped to her room, closing the door after her.

A minute later, Clay's head peeked around my door frame. "Noah sounds like a real jerk. What did he think was going to happen if he took them both?"

"I doubt he thought that far ahead."

"Truth. So, what do you want to do today?"

"You tell me. After all, you brought all the bags full of stuff."

Clay came closer and took my hand, tugging me up off my bed. "I have a couple different ideas. How special is this super-secret running spot you've been keeping from me?"

"Really special. But I don't want to jog today. I'll take you there, and we can play bocce ball or lawn bowling or whatever the game is called that's in your bag. And then we can come back here with donuts for Jenny. How does that sound?"

His smile warmed every part of me. "That sounds perfect."

If he didn't kiss me in the next three seconds I planned to remedy that, but then his phone rang, startling us both. Clay pulled it from his pocket and frowned, tilting the screen so I could see. It was Parker.

CHAPTER 23

CLAY

Of course, Lauren wanted to hear the conversation. It was like me talking to her dad while holding her all over again. Lauren's breath on my neck was quite distracting, along with her hands resting on my lower back, but I tuned her out the best I could and answered, trying to sound casual.

"Hey, Parker."

"Hey, where are you?"

I had to assume the question stemmed from him showing up at my house and not finding me there, or planning to go to my house, and in either case, I needed to decide where I was. "Running errands." It was as close to the truth as I could give him right now. I had filled up my gas tank on the way over, and I was now on my most important errand of the day—spending as much time as possible with Lauren.

"So, I had this idea. I got these broken-down four-wheelers for a song, and I thought it might make a good little niche business if we actually rented these out. You know, going into recreational equipment in addition to construction equipment. But I'd need your help seeing what all this entails before I tell John or Lauren I bought them. You can only imagine the grief she'd give me. I've worked on these types of engines a little bit, but you're better at cost and time breakdowns. I want to know the damage before I go into battle on this."

Why couldn't he just be asking to borrow money like a normal friend? I glanced at Lauren. She may have only caught half of what he said, but it was enough that her expression had turned wary. For the last little bit, we'd been living in a Clay and Lauren bubble, the type that could pop at any moment.

Well, I wasn't going to make the same mistake that Noah idiot did. I had my priorities straight for once, and if there was anything I'd learned from hearing Lauren's roommate storming in here, it was that you couldn't please everyone, and if you tried, it was a sure way to please no one.

"I can't today, Parker. But that does sound promising."

"Not at all today? What's going on?"

"I've sort of got a secret project of my own, and I can't tell you about it yet. But maybe I can help you work on those tomorrow?"

"Crap. What do I do with the four-wheelers until then? I was hoping to hide them in your garage."

Of course he was. I kept my garage clean and organized. It was something I was almost obsessive about. The last thing I wanted was a bunch of dead four-wheelers likely crawling with spiders parked in my space. Spiders loved the undersides of broken-down vehicles. You could almost hear their thinking. *I'll just live here since you're never getting around to this.* But compromises would have to be made.

"I have a key hidden in a fake rock behind the hibiscus bushes. Go put the four wheelers in my garage. But don't make a mess, okay? How many did you buy?"

"Five."

Five? I'd kill him later.

Lauren's eyes widened, and I shook my head at her. I knew the lecture she was dying to give. Heck, I had it memorized. So did Parker, not that it did any good.

After I hung up, I dropped my phone on the bed and pulled

her into me, hugging her tight. I wanted to kiss her so badly, but after her panic last night and the lackluster response she'd given to me telling her how I felt about her, I realized I needed to dial it in a little.

"You told him you had a secret project of your own," she murmured against my throat. I held in a groan. Her lips were like heat-seeking missiles. Or maybe mine were, and I had to change their trajectory before I got myself in trouble.

"At some point we have to tell him," I said, immediately regretting even saying that much. I felt her tense against me. "But not today. Let's go. Are you driving or am I?"

It was the perfect question to get her moving. Lauren had an unholy love for her truck. She immediately ran for her keys while I gathered up what we'd need.

She helped me carry everything down, and once we loaded up, I hopped in the passenger seat of her truck and put my seatbelt on. As much as I'd enjoy a tug-o-war over making me wear it, I wanted to show her my guard was down. Today, I wasn't Parker's annoying friend who liked to tease his little sister. Today, I was boyfriend material.

"Contemplating the universe over there?" Lauren asked, before starting up her truck.

"Something like that."

I paid attention to the route she took, trying to guess our destination, and I finally realized we were heading for Star Tower Park. I'd only ever been there once, to watch a friend's soccer match years ago.

It was a good running spot. Mature trees for shade, grassy hills, and not too crowded. She parked on the far side, away from the playground and skate park. We were lucky to have a bit of a breeze today, making it cooler than it would usually be this late in April.

I hopped out and retrieved my bags from the back of her truck. Lauren came over and relieved me of several of them, taking the opportunity to study what I'd brought while we walked. She fingered the thick quilt in the top of one of the bags. "What's this for?"

"Picnic?" I shrugged. "Don't you remember it from Fourth of July a couple of years ago? We played cards on it before the fireworks started."

Lauren thought for a moment. "I was with someone at the time, wasn't I?"

"Payson Grimes, the physical therapist. He didn't want to play cards so he just sat behind you and played with your hair."

Lauren stopped walking. "I'm not sure if I should be creeped out by that."

"Definitely creeped out. You couldn't see the expression on his face while he touched you." I grinned, knowing that wasn't what she meant. Although, I was totally not lying. Payson Grimes was a creep. Getting her to break up with him had been some of my finest work.

"Clay, I meant whether I should be creeped out by you holding onto those kind of details. Last I checked, you don't have a photographic memory."

"The fact that I remember the guy better than you says more about you than it does about me."

Lauren huffed out a breath and kept going, heading toward one of the large trees.

I lengthened my stride to keep up. "What would you like me to say?"

She shook her head. "I don't know. I'm just mad, I guess. And I'm not sure if I'm mad at you or me. Maybe it's a bit of both."

"Why would you be mad at yourself?"

"You said it, didn't you? What does it say about me? That I dated the creepy physical therapist, and he's barely a blip in my memory."

"The two of you only went out for a few weeks."

"You'd know." She elbowed me lightly but didn't back away. In fact, her head came to rest against my chest. "Why didn't you just ask me out yourself?" she murmured.

"You know why. It was easier to pretend I didn't want to."

She tilted her head to look up at me. "And scare away my

boyfriends?"

"I got pretty good at it."

"You told me Payson smelled like bacon when he sweated."

"Didn't he?"

She laughed, and then couldn't stop. "I couldn't un-smell it once you said it, and I was so mad at you. It was July in Phoenix! We were all sweating to death."

I couldn't put my arms around her with all the bags in my hands so I nudged her to keep us walking towards our destination.

We reached the tree, and I pulled the quilt out of the bag she was carrying, shaking it out until it unfolded and I could place it on the ground in the shade.

Lauren plopped down, crossing her tan legs in front of her. She had on a pair of khaki shorts that hit mid-thigh and a white blouse that billowed a little in the breeze, as did her hair, though it was pulled back into a loose ponytail.

"I do remember this quilt now. You told us we could never say a word to your Grandma about using it outside, because as far as she knows, you sleep with it every night."

"It's one step above tarp-level comfort. It's not meant for snuggling. She probably intended it that way."

Lauren tilted her head. "I can count on one hand the number of times I've heard you talk about your grandparents, and it's never with fondness."

Her words stabbed me, although I knew there was more curiosity on her side than reprimand.

"They're good people. I should talk better about them."

"When was the last time you saw them?"

"This morning. I was there at five mowing their lawn."

Lauren blinked. "Oh. Now I feel like a complete sloth for not being able to get out of bed at six."

"You're up early most days for work. Wanting to sleep in occasionally is not a crime. At least, not last I checked."

She fingered the corner of the quilt. "There are a lot of things about you that have always been none of my business, and therefore a mystery to me. Because you were Parker's best friend, and I was just his irritating sister hanging around."

As if she sensed the apology about to come out of my mouth, she held her hand up. "I'm not trying to call you out on it, I'm just... I don't know what I'm doing exactly."

"What about me is a mystery to you?"

She shook her head, backing away from the walls I already knew I was ready to let down.

I smiled and took her hand. "There's obviously something you're wondering about. Just say it."

"I've never seen the inside of the house you grew up in. Parker could go over there to get you, but not me."

"I think that was more about Parker being territorial than anything else, and maybe he was worried you'd ask something uncomfortable. It's not unheard of to live with your grandparents, but I did get asked about it a lot by other kids."

"I'm sorry about that."

"Would you like to?" I asked. It felt like the right thing to say, but my face started to heat at the thought.

"Would I like to what?" Lauren turned our clasped hands over and studied them, like the curious specimen they were. Holding her hand felt completely natural and yet very, very new.

"Go over there. To my grandparent's house."

"If you'd like me to, yes. And if not, that's okay, too."

"I don't really go visit them without a reason." I forced my jaw to relax so I wasn't gritting my teeth while trying to keep my hold on casual. This opening up thing had felt nice in theory. But pulling back the curtain and letting Lauren dig around and take a look made me feel a lot more exposed than I'd thought.

"Like needing to mow their lawn?"

"Yeah."

"What do they do for fun?"

I stared her down. My grandparents didn't believe in fun. It was my immediate reaction, and one I would have said aloud if Parker had asked, but Lauren watched me carefully, like she expected a real answer, so I gave it real thought.

"My grandmother reads the Reader's Digest magazine cover to cover. But nothing else. I tried buying her books for Christmas, but I don't think she read any of them. Grandpa likes to bird watch. Silently. I have a lot of memories of sitting next to him in a lawn chair for what felt like hours for one glimpse of a robin."

Lauren nodded. "That's right. Mom likes to bird watch, too. I think she and your grandpa talked about it once at a neighborhood watch meeting."

It was probably the one and only time the two of them had talked, but I didn't mention that.

"Do your grandparents have any hobbies they do together?" Lauren asked.

"They play Scrabble at night while they watch the news."

"Well, there you go. Have you ever played with them?"

I shook my head. Never. No way. They were ruthless scorekeepers, and would never have stopped to teach me the rules. I was a horrible speller anyway. Autocorrect and I were tight.

She got to her feet and tugged on my hand, probably sensing my discomfort. "We'll talk more while we play bocce."

I picked up the set and carried it over to a flat spot before tossing out the golf ball I used as a target about thirty feet in front of us.

Lauren tested the weight of one of the red balls from the set. "You'll be happy to know I'm horrible at this."

"Really? When was the last time you played?" I got out the green balls and dropped them at my feet.

"Um, on a date in high school. So I guess it's possible I've improved since then." She went first and rolled her ball about ten feet short of the target. "Never mind. I'm still horrible."

I rolled mine and knocked into her ball, sending it closer to the target while my ball bounced uselessly off to the side. I hadn't done it on purpose, but she turned and looked at me, completely appalled.

"What?" I asked.

"Don't let me win."

I stared her down. "Is that in the rules or something?"

"It's in my rules."

"I think you're giving me more credit than I deserve, and also less. I did not do that on purpose. I'm not sure I could if I tried."

"Oh." She turned an adorable shade of red. "My bad."

"Throw your next ball already." I nudged her with my hip, and she turned and threw her arms around me, burying her head in my chest.

"Are you hugging me or wrestling me?" I asked with a laugh.

"I haven't decided yet." She looked up, resting her chin on me. "This feels weird. Does it feel weird to you?"

"Which part?"

She let me go and picked up her ball, giving it a concentrated throw. It landed a lot closer to the target this time, but she didn't celebrate. "I don't know. Being out on what feels like a formal date with you. This point of no return." She bit her lip. "I'm overthinking again, aren't I?"

My stomach dropped, but I picked up my next ball, acting as if her words didn't bother me. "If you just want to be friends, it's okay. Or we could go back to hating each other. If that's what feels natural."

"Clay." Lauren said it like a reprimand.

"What?"

She took my hand and dragged me back to the tarp blanket. "Sit."

Great, another sit-down discussion. I already felt sliced open from the last one.

The second I was sitting, she climbed into my lap and took my face in her hands.

Her touch threw my senses into high alert. "I'm very confused right now." I closed my eyes, trying to lock down my feelings as her fingers skimmed across my neck and through the back of my hair.

"Clay, I don't want to backpedal. I don't want to hate you anymore. And I'm good with friendship as long as we get this, too." She kissed me, and with my eyes closed, all my focus went to the way it felt, the plumpness of her lips, the heat, the taste.

Two teenage girls walked by giggling, and Lauren scooted off my lap, wrapping her arms around her knees. We stared at each other and tried not to laugh. We'd totally just become *that* couple. The one nobody could take anywhere.

And then Lauren tensed again. A little wrinkle appeared in her forehead, and she reached out and covered my hand with hers. "Point of no return was a bad choice of words. I'm not worried about having a relationship with you. I'm worried it's not really what you want, and I can't seem to let go of that fear. I can't help testing you to see if you're gonna wink at me and take it all back."

"Go back to teasing you like I used to?"

"Yeah."

"I guess I deserve that."

"You don't. And I've been nosy about your grandparents for no reason at all. I feel like we need a do-over."

"No do-overs. Things are going to be weird. For a lot of reasons." Like her dad, and Parker, and being coworkers. The ownership thing we still hadn't talked about. But right then wasn't the time to get into all that. "I think what we need is a friendly wager to make this game more interesting. If I lose, I'll call up my grandparents and tell them we'd like to come over and play Scrabble." Maybe Lauren and I could play as a team. I was familiar enough with her precise note-taking to know she was probably good at word games.

"And if *I* lose?" She bit her lip. We both knew, chances were pretty good I'd be cashing in.

"If you lose, you won't freak out over Parker buying all those four wheelers with company money."

"It's another bad business decision. I can't offer up how I feel about it on a bet. In fact, I've been thinking about this a lot. You and Parker should change positions at work."

That took me aback. "Wait, what?"

"You should take over acquisitions. He should stick to

maintenance and repair."

"Have you told him this?"

"Of course not. I figured I'd introduce the idea to the less stubborn of the two of you and go from there."

"He'd see it as a step down in position, you know. He already does repair. All you want to do is cut his purse strings and hand them over to me."

"I know." She deflated, and I pulled her into me. As hard as it was to work with friends, it had to be a lot harder to work with family. "That's why I haven't brought it up, even though I've thought about it for years."

"So, back to our wager. What are you offering if you lose?"

"You get to drive home?" she asked.

Ah, her magical truck. I'd have fun with that. "Deal."

We started our game over, with Lauren throwing the target this time. She tossed the golf ball a lot lighter than me, which would be to her advantage. Or so she thought. My short game was pretty good, and I took the round, getting two points for being closest, and one point for second closest.

Lauren was focused though, and even though I tossed the target farther on the next round, she gave it her all and took all the points, tying us up at three.

When we were tied at ten to ten, I really started to get nervous. We were only playing to twelve.

"Watching you sweat over this is a reward in and of itself." Lauren bounced up on her toes as I took my next turn.

My ball veered left and just kept going. My second ball fell short. Not good. Lauren would have to choke or it was over.

Unfortunately, she learned from my mistake and tossed her ball a little to the right to miss the dip in the grass my ball had fallen into. She was taking first place. She threw her second ball and it skimmed passed my short one and kept going until it hugged the target. First and second. Thirteen points to my ten.

CHAPTER 24

LAUREN

I ran upstairs to my apartment with donuts for Jenny while Clay waited downstairs in the truck. I had told him several times I wouldn't hold him to our bet, but he was a man of his word and had called his grandparents and asked if we could come over. In a show of support, I'd let him drive my truck despite my win. Except for peeling out of the parking lot just to tick me off, he'd treated my metal baby very well.

I found Jenny in the kitchen, working out her feelings through culinary means. Whenever she had something on her mind, she cooked or baked. We were both enthusiastic leftover eaters, so it worked out well. And occasionally, when her creations got out of hand, we brought some to the neighbors in our building. The old guy who lived next door did not like chitchat, but he loved Jenny's stir-fry.

"You're back early. And without Clay. Dare I ask?" Jenny dried her hands and came over to see what type of donuts I'd brought. Clay and I had devoured half a dozen between the two of us, but we'd left Jenny the chocolate flavored cake donuts I knew were her favorites.

"He's waiting in my truck. Are you okay?"

"Couldn't be better. I forgot I'd preordered a book from my favorite author, and it showed up today in my reading app. As soon as this dough is ready to rise, I'm going to dive into it."

"Good, because I don't know when I'll be back."

"Really? I'm liking the sound of that, sister." She slapped my butt with a kitchen towel and ran before I could retaliate. "I want to hear it all later."

"Sure, sure." Assured she'd be fine, I hurried back downstairs so Clay and I could drive over to his grandparents. He had made no promises on what type of visit it would be. Usually, his grandma would hint when it was time for him to go, and that was that. It broke my heart a little, to hear him talk about it so matter-of-factly. The few times I had interacted with his grandma in the past had not been unfriendly, but had definitely not been friendly either. I wasn't sure if she was purposefully intimidating or if it just came naturally to her.

Clay had moved to the passenger side while I was gone, so I jumped into the driver's seat and adjusted the rearview mirror before running my hands lovingly over the steering wheel, silently apologizing for letting someone else drive it. When I looked at Clay, he was smirking.

"How come I don't get a greeting like that?"

"Jealous?"

"Clearly."

My eyes roved over him, taking in everything that made him so attractive. His mischievous smile, his tall and lean body. No wonder Denise Perkins wanted a piece of this. "Did you ever call Denise?"

Clay's shoulders sank. "Our minds are clearly in different places right now. No, I didn't call her, but only because she called me first. I told her I was sorry, but I started seeing someone. And then she pinned me down on dates and times until I either had to admit it was you or pretend it was an old crush who finally gave me the time of day. Technically, both of those are true."

"So, you told her it was me?"

"Heck no. You'd gain a stalker. Plus, word would get back to Melissa."

"True. I hadn't thought about that." I wondered what Melissa would think of the two of us together. She'd probably be mad she hadn't thought of it first.

"How is Jenny?" Clay asked, sliding across the bench seat and invading my space. I shivered in anticipation as he leaned in, his deep grey-blue eyes staring into mine. His lips were so close, yet not close enough. "Lauren?"

"What?" I ran my hand over his biceps. Why weren't we kissing yet?

"How's your roommate? Was she okay?"

Oh, right. He'd asked me a question. I smoothed the front of his shirt as if ridding it of the imaginary wrinkles I'd placed there when I'd grabbed it inside my short-lived fantasy. "She's fine. Jenny's not one to let anything get her down for long. Besides, she's been shipping the two of us since the day you showed up to drive me to work when my truck was acting up. She practically shooed me back out the door just now."

"Shipping?"

"Yeah, like when you want two people to get together because you sense something the two of them don't see, you ship them. Relation*ship*." My hands went back to his biceps under the hems of his short-sleeved tee. His muscles were smooth and warm. Way nicer than the leather of my steering wheel. *Sorry, truck. Still love you.*

I leaned in and kissed one of his biceps and then immediately felt really stupid. It was like my brain had short circuited and my lips had been put in charge of decision-making. I laughed nervously. "I don't know why I did that I—"

Clay's mouth closed on mine. "Don't." Another kiss. "Worry." More kissing. "About it."

Kissing him was like the sun warming my back on a winter day, like hitting the gas pedal on a long empty stretch of freeway. I wrapped my arms around his back and held on.

Eventually, though, we were abruptly reminded that we were in an apartment complex parking lot. We both turned and looked through the driver's side window to see the guy who had pulled into the spot next to us. Staring. Smiling. I wanted to swing open my driver door and dent his car, but I wisely refrained. Clay and I really did need to pick better places to make out.

"To my grandparents' house," Clay said with a groan, slowly letting me go. He stayed in the middle seat as I put the truck into drive. I liked his thigh right up next to mine, which I knew was no accident on his part. I think we both needed the continual physical contact, a promise we were in this for real, and neither of us would back out.

"We don't have to go to your grandparents if you don't want to. Like you said earlier, today's just about spending as much time together as possible before…" I paused.

"Before your dad gets back." He finished my sentence of dread.

"He wants Parker and I to sign something saying we won't date employees once we're part owners."

"Are you serious?"

"Yes, but I'm not going to do that."

"It makes sense in a way."

"No. Don't even defend it." I gripped his knee. "I know I've sent you mixed, panicked signals, but it's because I've been getting used to the idea of us, not because I don't want it. I'm actually a little scared of how much I want it." I took in a deep breath and blew it out. In every previous relationship, I'd avoided big feelings, and especially, admitting to having them. Denver had told me I was hard to read. I would go further and say I was hard to reach.

Clay nudged my shoulder. "I'm here for whatever kind of signals you want to send, baby."

"That's the worst pickup line I've ever heard." But I was secretly grateful for it. He knew me well enough not to push too hard. I needed time to think. If Clay was what I'd wanted all along, why was I still locked in my protective shell, afraid to open up to him? Was it just habit?

No. I looked over at him, sitting in the middle seat while I drove, which some guys would have considered emasculating. Clay wasn't just some guy. He was *the* guy. Mine. I wanted him for keeps. And that was scary. Everything went back to my fear. Before, I'd been cautious, maybe even callous. But now, I was terrified of how much I liked him and what upheaval it would cause to both our lives to pursue this.

"So, where am I going?"

"To my grandparents. Unless you want to die. Once you tell them you're coming, you show up, or else."

"Well, if death is on the line, by all means, let's go play some Scrabble."

"I don't know about the Scrabble thing."

"Bird watching then."

"Or coupon clipping."

I nodded. "Coupon clipping. I'm down with that."

"Judging the neighbors for leaving out their garbage can."

"Clay."

He laughed. "Mockery is my love language."

"Well, that explains some things."

His playful mood lasted until we turned onto our block, and then we both got quiet. I parked in front of his grandparent's house, but my eyes were on my parents' house not too far down the street. My mom would be home. I wouldn't even mind her knowing about us. Maybe she already suspected. Maybe she could help prep my dad.

Clay lightly squeezed my knee. "I know what you're thinking. You want to tell her."

"Not today. Your grandparents are waiting." That, and I wanted to call her first. Surprises weren't really Mom's thing. Or mine, for that matter.

I opened my door and slid out, and Clay took my hand as we walked up to the door. His hand in mine felt so nice, I had to hold back the tears threatening to pop out. That never happened. What was wrong with me?

"Anything else I should know?" I asked, suddenly nervous. What would his grandparents think of the two of us together? Forget what I'd said. I wasn't ready for anyone else to know yet.

"I've never brought a girlfriend to meet them. No pressure."

"Am I your girlfriend?" I blurted out.

He'd been about to knock but he dropped his hand. "Are you?"

"I don't know. Last I checked, there wasn't a protocol for this sort of thing."

Clay laughed. "Are you afraid of labels, Lauren?"

"No." I squeezed his hand. "Okay, I'm your girlfriend."

"Good." He locked eyes with me.

"Good."

The door opened before I could kiss his face off.

His grandma stood there with her kitchen broom in hand. I wasn't sure if she'd been sweeping, or if it was just part of her intimidating look. "What are you standing there for? I could hear you talking but you never knocked." She looked at him before her eyes rested on me. Studying me. "Parker's sister." She looked at our clasped hands and her eyebrows raised as if to say, *interesting*.

"This is Lauren, Grandma."

"Yes, I see that. Come in. Are we really playing Scrabble? You've never wanted to before, Clayton."

"Whatever you'd like to do, Grandma."

I followed the direction of his gaze over to a scary-looking Nutcracker doll on the mantle across the room. It was like the eye of Sauron as far as he was concerned. I could just tell. Maybe I could accidentally knock it over and break it on our way out. Except I wanted to make a good first impression. Dang it.

His Grandma motioned to the table. "Well, I have the game set up. Or we could play Password instead."

"No, Scrabble is fine," Clay said quickly, leading me into the kitchen.

"What's Password?" I whispered.

"Worse than Scrabble. All I know is it involves a long staring contest and one word answers. They play it for hours."

"You're a Harwood, aren't you?" Clay's grandpa stood when we came in and reached out to shake my hand.

"Yep. I sure am."

"That's enough chitchat. Let's play." Clay's grandma sank into the seat across from us and took her seven letter pieces from the pile, placing them on her wooden rack. Clay was not joking. When it came to game playing, she meant serious business.

On the ride over, we had agreed to play as a team, but one frown from Clay's grandma was all it took for him to take his own rack and place letters on it. Admitting to me he was intimidated by the game had been humbling enough. Now he was tossed into what I knew would be a cut-throat game, and it was all my fault. I took a peek at his letters, swapping them around in my mind while his grandparents took their turns.

I nudged his foot with mine before saying, "That bridge closure sure was a pain."

"Yep. Lots of traffic." I was so glad he'd gone along with my weird statement, because otherwise he'd totally give away my blatant attempt to help him. Unfortunately, one look from him was all it took to know he had no idea what I was doing.

There was an E available for his use at the end of his grandfather's word, and he had B, R, I, D, and G sitting there, waiting to be used. I nudged his foot again and looked right at his letters.

And then he got it. He placed them on the board, and took his respectable points. I went next, smiling at his grandma who had continued to study me with interest. Interest was better than contempt. Interest, I could deal with. It meant they cared about Clay, and I wanted them to care about him. There was no one in the world who deserved to be loved more than him.

I picked up the hand loose at his side and rested it on my knee, and then began tracing letters into his palm before each of his turns. MIFFED. TOXIC. JULEP. I was concentrating so hard on helping him that I was losing, by a lot.

"Are you left-handed, Lauren?" Clay's grandma asked after jotting down her triple word score. She stared me down, and it was like she was gazing into my soul.

"No. I'm just holding Clay's hand."

"Why?"

"Because I like him."

"Clay, what does miffed mean?"

I bit my lip and glanced over at him. We were so busted.

He squeezed my hand. "Miffed means you're upset?"

"Use it in a sentence."

"Grandma is miffed because someone dropped something toxic in her mint julep."

There was this awkward silence right after where laughter should have been. Like a stand-up comedian telling fart jokes at a women's country club meeting.

His grandma's eyes narrowed. "If someone tried to poison me, I'd be pretty miffed. Almost as miffed as I'd be if someone cheated while playing Scrabble with me."

"Yes, ma'am."

I echoed him, and for a half second, I saw a ghost of a smile cross her face. It was so brief I wondered if I'd imagined it.

She turned to her husband. "Did you know they were cheating?"

"Since bridge," Clay's grandfather acknowledged in that quiet, gravelly voice of his.

"And you weren't going to say anything?"

The old man shrugged. "In my house growing up, if you didn't cheat at cards, you weren't trying hard enough."

"Have you ever cheated while we've played?"

"No, ma'am. I didn't want anything toxic dropped in my anything."

"Harold." Clay's grandma shook her head, but that ghost of a smile was back, less ghostly this time and much more alive.

Clay stared at his grandparents like he'd never seen them before. I was pretty sure his grandpa didn't say much of anything on a good day and never made jokes. Had that been a joke just now?

Suddenly aware we were watching them and their cute interaction, Clay's grandma waved her hands at us, shooing us back to our letter tiles. "Whose turn is it?"

"Mine," I admitted. I put down QUAKE on a triple word score and suddenly I was back in the game.

CHAPTER 25

CLAY

So much about Saturday changed everything. My grandparents were... I didn't know how to describe it. They were people I wanted to hang out with, mostly because for the first time ever, I felt like they were okay with me hanging around. I could go back and study every bit of our history and make tally marks of blame in different columns, but I think it came down to this: the ice had been broken.

"You were a big part of it," I told Lauren late Sunday night on the phone as I was explaining my theory. The weekend of us was coming to a close, and I was afraid to let it go. Monday mornings were not traditionally known for awesomeness.

"I didn't do anything except get you in trouble. Is that what it was? You did something your grandma didn't approve of and realized it was going to be okay?"

"More like I realized what I'd been missing. They have secret personalities I never got to see. I don't think they did it on purpose. It was just the generation of 'children should be seen and not heard.' I feel like I've finally been initiated into a secret club for grownups."

"Well, I'm glad, Clay. I'm glad my nosiness about them didn't end up being a complete disaster."

"It didn't." I stifled a yawn. It was twelve-thirty, and I had left her apartment a half-hour ago. I'd been up since four.

In order to have time with her the rest of Sunday, I had woken up Parker at the crack of dawn and made him come over to inspect the piece of crap four-wheelers he'd left in my garage. And they were pieces of crap. Three of them had only needed a tune-up to be moderately worthless toys that were too old for most serious riders to be interested in. The other two? Their engines were shot and would need a complete rebuild. He had overpaid by every stretch of the imagination. Even with us doing all the work ourselves, we'd be lucky to break even on the whole project.

As if Lauren could read my mind, she asked. "How did it go with Parker today? You totally changed the subject when I asked earlier."

"I know I did. Because I don't want to talk about it."

"Because of the ATVs?"

"Because of a lot of things. He pulled one of your long blonde hairs off my shoulder. It was clinging to my shirt. And he had questions about it."

Lauren gasped. "No. How was it still there?"

"I rolled out of bed in what I'd worn the night before, which I guess included a little token from you." Not that I could put all the blame on her. I was the one who liked to run my fingers through her hair.

"What did you tell Parker?"

"I made up this completely bogus story about my dryer going out and taking my clothes to a laundromat. Worst cover story ever. Especially after he offered to look at my dryer, and I said it was already fixed. Luckily, Parker's a good enough friend he let me be. But now he knows I'm dating some mystery woman I don't want to talk about."

She sighed a melancholy sigh. "We should go to bed."

"I know."

But neither of us ended the call.

"Clay?"

"Yeah."

"I'm anxious."

"About tomorrow?"

"Yeah." But the way she said it told me she was anxious about every tomorrow.

"If you can't do this, it's okay, you know?" I hated that I felt like I had to keep saying that.

"Nope." Lauren was quick to squash that train of thought, much to my relief. "No outs. I'm not giving you one. You're not giving me one. You're a part of my life, and you always have been. We've just tweaked things slightly."

"'We've just tweaked things slightly?' Is that going into the speech you've prepared for your dad? I don't think he'll go with that logic."

"Whatever. I don't have anything prepared. I'm still dwelling on how to end this call with you."

"Okay, explain."

Lauren gave a nervous laugh. "Well, you were the one who said, 'I like you' first. And I'm not ready for the other four letter L word yet. Is there something in-between people say?"

I rubbed my forehead. This girl. The first rule of commitment issues: you didn't talk about your commitment issues. Unless you were Lauren. "You already know I'm bad at Scrabble. Now you want me to come up with a four letter word that's in between like and love?"

"It doesn't have to be four letters or start with L. For example, don't British people say, I fancy you? What about that?"

"I'm pretty sure they don't say it at the end of phone calls. Ta ta, I fancy you."

She snorted. "Okay, what then?"

"Lauren, you are beautiful and weird, and I really like you. And I hope tomorrow doesn't end in your dad wanting to punch me. Now go to bed, sweetheart." I hung up before she spent another thirty minutes crafting an appropriate response.

CHAPTER 26

LAUREN

Poor Parker was getting asked about his plans a lot. I think it was getting into his head because just our asking was causing him to make plans so he wouldn't look like a loser. He had no idea all we wanted to know was the probability of him showing up unannounced at Clay's front door.

I liked hanging out at Clay's house. I liked dancing in his kitchen. And I liked planning our lunch schedules so we took different routes to the same cozy picnic bench. I'd never felt this way about anyone before, where instead of getting increasingly stressed out over the relationship progressing, I couldn't wait to see him. Clay was the best part of my day, whether we were talking on the phone, or eating together, or he was kissing me goodnight on my doorstep in-between yawns. I really needed to let him get more sleep.

So far, the business hadn't encroached on our relationship at all. But I knew it was coming. I hadn't spoken up about anything in our company meeting on Tuesday, which was very unlike me. I didn't butt heads with Parker in the warehouse. I was trying to stay off everyone's radar. But things couldn't go on in limbo forever.

We had an ownership meeting I'd successfully put off until next Monday. All I had to do was get through Friday unscathed and we'd have another weekend together without any work nonsense messing it up. I must have jinxed myself because I knew something was wrong the second the front office called me. A tingly thread of unease ran up my back.

"There's a large flower bouquet up here for you," the secretary, Paisley, said, with more than a hint of amusement in her voice. "And the sender would love to see you if you have the time. He's talking to your dad right now."

"Who's talking to my dad?"

"I think his name is Nibble, but I was too afraid to ask again. It's not really Nibble, is it?"

"Oh, no." I hung up and sprang to my feet. Crappity crap crap. This was not good.

Clay glanced my way from across the warehouse when I walked past, but I gave a little shake of my head. Now was not the time for secret meetups, however much I might want that. Today was supposed to be about laying low, not dealing with insane ex-dates.

I jogged into the front office building and opened the back door with the stealth of a practiced ninja, ducking down behind a desk and surveying the situation. Noble and my Dad were shooting the breeze at the counter in front of the receptionist desk while Paisley listened in.

The flower bouquet perched on the end of the counter was loud and exotic and fragrant. Lilies and birds of paradise sprung out in every direction. I was so not carrying it back to my desk. It would take up the whole space and everyone would stop and ask about it. That was the purpose, wasn't it? Noble had sent flowers as a statement. An attention grabber. He wanted me to know he was a nice guy who did nice things, not a guy who got ditched at the end of an awkward date. This was about wrapping things up with me in a nice, tidy bow. Well, that, or I had a go-getter stalker. How I handled things now depended a lot on reading his motives right.

"What are you doing?"

I about jumped out of my skin and turned around, grabbing the lapels of Parker's shirt and dragging him down to my level.

"Keep your voice down, idiot."

"Is this about the flowers? Who's that guy talking to Dad?"

"Noble Tuttle, my date from last weekend."

"So things went well." Parker grinned at me.

"No, they did not."

"Then why is he here?"

"That's what I'm trying to figure out."

Parker stood and pointed down at me, calling out, "She's over here."

I stomped on his foot, not that it did any good with his steel-toe boots, and walked over to face the music with as much dignity as I could muster. Parker, being the worst brother ever, had already slinked out the back door now that he'd outed me from my hiding spot. In all fairness, he had also given me the push I needed, but I would definitely not be thanking him. No, quite the opposite. Vengeance would be mine.

My face was flaming red as I smiled at Noble. I could feel the heat of it. "Hi, Noble. Thank you for the flowers."

"Oh, it was nothing," he said with fake humility, letting his eyes linger on the tropical arrangement with obvious pride. "I just felt like maybe we got off on the wrong foot with our date, and I'd like to try again. I was hoping I could take you to lunch right now. Your dad here was saying this is usually when you take your lunch break."

"That's very kind of you, but, no thank you. I need to get back to work."

Noble's eyebrows dipped. "But your dad said it was okay. He said you can go right now." Noble had the audacity to turn to my dad, as if expecting him to over-rule me.

To my relief, Dad pointed back at me. "Noble, she's kindly said no. If the two of you want to arrange for another time, that's up to her." He walked back towards his office, although I knew he'd be listening to see how this train wreck ended.

Noble took in a deep breath and blew it out. "Is there another time that works better?"

I shook my head. "Sorry, no." I couldn't pretend another time might work. Noble needed a clear message, not subtlety.

"But I brought you flowers," he huffed, looking at the bouquet once again. I could see the numbers adding up in his mind. Time. Money. Ego. The investment wasn't paying off the way he'd expected.

"I know. I'm sorry."

"They were really expensive."

"Would you like to take them back?" I hadn't meant it flippantly, but it still surprised me when he carefully picked up the heavy vase and held it close to his chest.

"I'll take them to my mother."

As he stalked out the door, I noticed one of the lilies brushed against his shoulder, leaving a smudge of orange pollen across the white of his shirt. It looked like he'd been hugged by a toddler eating Cheetos. This was not going to be his day.

"Lauren," my dad called out from his office. "I want to talk to you."

Apparently, it wasn't going to be mine either. I ignored Paisley's stare and headed to my dad's office, shutting the door behind me.

He shook his head and smiled. "I don't even know where to start. I'm not sure if I should apologize for setting you up with that guy, or if Melissa should."

I sat in the chair across from his desk. "I'll take an apology from you. They're so rare."

He raised an eyebrow in an I'll-allow-it sort of way. "You know this kind of thing is exactly why I want a no-dating policy."

"For all the employees, or is this still an ownership thing?"

"An ownership thing. The balance of power it creates is so much worse than unwanted flowers. So, are you willing to sign the no-dating-employees clause or not?"

I knew this had been coming, and I still panicked. "Did you know Parker bought a bunch of four wheelers last weekend on company money?"

Dad's face turned red. "He did what?" He picked up his phone and dialed Parker's extension. "Get in my office. Now." When his eyes turned back to me, I knew I wasn't off the hook. Actually, I had made a much bigger mess, as I wasn't supposed to know about the four wheelers in Clay's garage. Crap. Had I just mixed him up in all this, too?

"Stay right there." Dad got up from his desk, and I ducked my head out after he left to see him taking over Paisley's computer, probably to check the business account and see exactly how much money he needed to yell at Parker about.

Someone grabbed my shoulders from behind, and I jumped in shock.

Parker laughed. "Gotcha."

His enjoyment of once again getting the drop on me only lasted until Dad's head popped up above Paisley's computer screen to glare at us.

"He knows about the four wheelers," I whispered.

Parker sighed. "I was going to report it, obviously. It's not like I didn't know accounting would catch up with me about it eventually."

"But you were hoping to sell them first?"

"Maybe."

We went to sit back in Dad's office, and he came back in, staring down each of us in turn. "Owners don't buy things without consulting the other owners first. That's the rule from now on."

"Does that go for you, too?" Parker asked.

"Of course."

"Every expense?"

"Don't try to turn this around on me. Filling up for gas? No. Taking a client to lunch, no. Four-thousand in equipment? Absolutely. I should fire you. If you were anyone else, I would. So decide if you really want to be an owner. It's a different mindset than owner's son, and if you don't understand the difference, we're done here."

Parker ducked his head. "I'm sorry. It won't happen again. I promise."

I bit my lip. Parker meant it. For all his faults, he didn't make empty promises. Usually he didn't make promises at all. Or apologies, for that matter.

Dad cleared his throat. "I've been thinking about what Lauren said in our last meeting. I'd like to invite Clay to be an owner."

I felt so many emotions all at once. Relief, excitement, worry, and fear. Bringing Clay in had felt like a much better idea when I could deny we had a relationship. We sure had one now, one we weren't in any hurry to disclose.

Parker looked relaxed, but his hands were gripping the arms of his chair. He was working through his own mixed emotions about it. I could tell. "How would that work?"

"You, Lauren, Clay, and Mom would each get fifteen percent. I would keep forty percent until I'm ready to retire, and then just like we talked about, Mom and I would distribute our shares back to you. The three of you in this case."

"And does Clay know yet?" Parker asked.

"No. I needed you two to agree to it first. After all, it's sharing your cut. Lauren, is that still something you want?"

I nodded, not trusting myself to say more.

"What about you, Parker?"

He nodded as well. "Clay's family. I can share my cut."

Dad leaned forward and rested his elbows on the desk. "Now, getting back to the question I asked Lauren. Owners cannot date employees of this company. I don't want any favors, messy breakups, or possible liability."

Parker held his hands up. "I already said I'd sign."

Dad turned to me. "I know Clay will, too. Lauren, what's holding you back?"

"Nothing." I thought about the terms owner and employee. Nothing in it would say owners couldn't date each other. It was a big logical leap, but it was the only one available to me, so I'd take it. "Fine. I'll sign."

Dad dismissed us, and I got back to work. Every time Clay looked at me, I felt hot and cold all over, and not just because of what the man did to my senses. I felt torn. I knew ownership was what Clay wanted deep down. But if I warned him it was coming, what would he say? I had a feeling he would turn it down. He wouldn't see my logical leap as logical, but a trap we were setting for ourselves. But if the offer came from my dad? My dad would be a lot harder to say no to. Somehow, pulling myself out of telling him the news seemed like the right thing to do.

CHAPTER 27

CLAY

"I want you to be an owner with Lauren and Parker." The words registered over and over in my mind while I inwardly panicked over the timing. Trying to read John's body language didn't help. The man had always been unflappable. Unless he was yelling. Right now, I couldn't tell if he was happy to share the news with me or just resigned to it.

"What does that mean, exactly?" I picked at the oil in the crease of my fingernail. I should be thanking him, but all I wanted was to know when this had been decided, and by whom. Was this why Lauren had come back from the office and avoided my eyes? She knew. She knew, and she hadn't said anything.

A flash of irritation mixed with attraction flooded over me. That woman. She was trouble, the sort of trouble that would keep me on my toes for years to come. Well, if we didn't go down in a blaze of glory. How could I share ownership with her and not disclose we were dating? I was standing in front of her father.

I was standing in front of her father. At that moment, I couldn't even look him in the eyes, knowing what he would do to me if he knew about us.

"What it means is you'll get a share just like Lauren and Parker. I want you to know they're both on board with this. We know this company means just as much to you as it does to us."

"Thank you, sir." I'd probably have to turn him down, but I just couldn't yet. I needed to think. I needed to talk to Lauren and find out what exactly had happened and what the two of us were supposed to do about it.

But that conversation would have to wait. I sat there patiently while John pulled out paperwork and figures and talked about the details and his future plans for the company. We talked about equipment purchases and the cap he'd put on spending, mostly because of Parker, although he didn't outright say it. Ownership would officially seal the end of Parker's secret purchases. Lauren would be thrilled.

"So, Lauren and Parker will be here any minute, along with Barry, who is creating the contracts."

"They will?" I jumped to my feet, realizing this meeting was a precursor to an ownership meeting I hadn't given much thought to, except as part of Lauren's schedule. Now it was part of mine, and I hadn't even decided if I wanted this, and more importantly, if I could even have it.

"Where are you going?" John asked.

"The bathroom. Sorry. I'll be right back." I dashed out of there and turned the corner, only to almost run Lauren over. I put my arms out to keep her from falling back, and they naturally threaded around her waist of their own accord, resting on the small of her back. At least, until my brain caught up and registered that Parker was standing right next to us, staring.

I drew my arms back and looked away. "Sorry. Just running to the bathroom." Darting around them, I locked myself in the tiny office bathroom and went into full-on panic mode.

I finally understood how Lauren had felt when faced with big decisions and paperwork that would make it binding. This was all too much. Wasn't it?

The stress began to ebb a little, making room for excitement. I was finally a part of them, the Harwood family. They wanted me to help take the business into the future, something I'd always wanted to do. I had been so focused on Lauren, I'd forgotten everything else about my future. Yes, we'd have to tell them we were dating, but our relationship was so new, it didn't have to be now. We'd figure out the right time to speak up.

I washed my hands and splashed water on my face, drying it off on a scratchy paper towel and then quickly fixing my hair, which instead of looking strategically messy, was giving off a crazed stress-case vibe. Taking a deep breath, I walked out with confidence I didn't quite feel and returned to John's office.

They had borrowed a few chairs from the conference room while I'd been gone, and I took a seat between Parker and Lauren. Barry, the accountant, was sitting by the window.

"How are you feeling?" John asked.

"I'm a little freaked out, to be honest."

Everyone laughed, though there was a nervous edge to it. I didn't dare look at either Parker or Lauren. John smiled like he understood my position. He had no idea.

"We're all friends here, and I'd like to say we knew exactly what we were doing from the beginning, but there are about a hundred ways to go about a business hand-off, and some are better than others. Am I right, Barry?"

Barry looked up from his computer. "Yes. But we're going to come up with the best transfer plan for everybody with clear steps until John is eventually phased out of the daily operations. You know, when he's a hundred and five and can't drive his motorized scooter in here anymore."

John looked a lot less amused than the joke called for, and Barry went back to studying his computer, saying, "Go ahead, John. I'll stop you when anything needs a further explanation."

That was all the introduction John needed. "Right, well, let's talk about the business shares."

"GRATs," Barry clarified. "Grantor retained annuity trusts. It's better than annual gifting. There are more fees involved, but less taxes paid."

Parker had about a hundred follow-up questions, while Lauren and I did our best not to look at each other. Her fidgety hands told me everything I needed to know. She was as nervous as I was.

"Parker, I know you feel like we've already hashed this out, but it needs to be brought up again. The four-wheeler purchase. Even if you had found them at a good deal and they were one-hundred percent for the company and not personal use, that's a unilateral decision to branch out into power sport rentals like RVs and boats and recreational vehicles. We don't do that. Our customer base is completely different."

Parker scowled. "I get it. I was wrong on multiple levels."

"I'm just saying. If Lauren hadn't mentioned it to me, when exactly were you going to tell me about it?"

Parker sat up. "Wait, Lauren told you about the four-wheelers?"

Lauren's face turned three shades of guilty, and she shot me an apologetic look, one Parker caught. This was just getting better and better.

Parker didn't look angry anymore, he looked contemplative. He stared from Lauren to me and then back to Lauren. "The four wheelers are in Clay's garage. He and I were the only ones who knew about them."

"You used a company credit card," Lauren shot back, but her face, which had never told a lie, was betraying her in bright, red, hyper color. Her eyes darted to mine again. Now was not the time to look to me for comfort.

Parker shot from his chair and stared me down. "You told her about the four wheelers. That blonde hair on your shoulder on Sunday morning was hers, wasn't it? And I swear I saw Lauren's truck down the street from your house the other night, when you were supposedly off doing errands for your grandparents. You've been doing a lot of errands lately. The cookies!" Parker swung around and pointed back at Lauren. "You were there that night, weren't you?"

"Will someone please tell me what is going on?" John

banged on his desk, and Parker whirled around to face him.

"Lauren and Clay are secretly dating."

It suddenly got really quiet. Barry shut his computer with a snap and stood. "John, I'm gonna go. Call me later." The man sent me a look of quiet empathy before walking out the door and closing it behind him.

This was not going to end well. Not that I regretted any of it except for the timing. I made the mistake of conveying my lack of regret to Lauren in one brief smoldering look. I needed her to know I didn't blame her. Her terrible lack of deceit was one of the things I liked best about her. She raised her eyebrows back at me like I'd lost my mind. Maybe I had.

We were interrupted by John smacking his desk again. "What exactly has been going on between you two?"

"That's why she didn't want to sign a no-dating policy. She was already breaking it." Parker stared at us, suddenly looking suspicious. "And Lauren was the one who suggested we add Clay as an owner. It was her idea. How exactly did that come about?"

Just like that, the temperature in the room dropped fifty degrees.

John locked eyes with me. I felt all his mistrust and all the insinuations Parker was making. And it hurt. A lot. It was rejection. And not belonging. And feeling like a guest in your own house. This was my work home and they were my family. I was safe here. Or so I'd thought. I could take anger, and I could take surprise. But this... I didn't want to look at Lauren. I didn't want her pity, or worse, to see her question my motives along with them. I didn't want her torn between choosing them or me. I never should have put her in that position.

For several long seconds, I warred with whether to explain myself, but it all felt so humiliating. I sighed, letting out something I thought I'd never say. "Don't worry. I quit."

I turned to go, but Lauren jumped up and blocked the door before I could leave it. "Stop it. Just stop it," she pled. "Nobody say another word that can't be taken back."

Too late for that. I couldn't stay. Damage control would have to be a Harwood affair, and I wasn't a Harwood. I gently moved Lauren's arm out of the way, avoiding her pleas to stay, and ran.

It was the first time I'd ever ditched work. I'd given everything to this place, but for the next few hours, I didn't want to think about any of it. I texted Evan to let him know which skid steers still needed oil changes, and then I powered down my phone and drove off.

CHAPTER 28

LAUREN

It didn't take Dad long to recover from his shock. As soon as Clay left, he launched into a long-winded lecture about how this was just like what happened with Boyce, and how he couldn't believe I could do something like this to the company. Again.

But this was nothing like Boyce. Yes, Boyce had been a good guy, and probably a good fit for me. But I hadn't loved him enough because I hadn't allowed myself to.

I hadn't trusted him with my whole heart because I was too afraid of what might happen if I let someone in. If people couldn't see the real me, then they couldn't judge me, and they couldn't control that part of me, and my feelings were safe. But there was loneliness in surface relationships, and it took Clay coaxing more out for me to see it.

I did feel more with him. Jenny had been more right than she'd realized.

"How could you not see this coming?" Dad asked, dropping into his desk chair and putting his head in his hands. "Lauren, what were you thinking?"

I had to stop checking the hallway for Clay. He wasn't coming back, and the only one out there was Paisley, who was surely listening in. Whatever, I was past caring who knew our business. I'd go and make things right with Clay, but not until I'd cleaned up the mess here. And, boy, was it a mess.

I turned around in the doorway to face my dad. My body shook with the control it took not to lose it completely. "This time is different, Dad. This time, I quit, too. I'm so ashamed of this family. Clay has never done anything to betray your trust before. Except fall for me. And for your information, I thought about Clay having part ownership before we started dating. I told him so, and he brushed me off. In fact, he forbid me from saying anything, but I did it anyway. Because I'm a Harwood and we're a bunch of hotheads."

I turned to Parker, who was squirming. I was about to make him squirm even more. "Did you really just tell your best friend you think he's trying to weasel favor in the company through me? That is not only stupid, it's cruel. Yeah, he lied to you about us, but that doesn't change you being a bad friend. And Dad, the night Clay and I got together was the night of my double date with Noble. I found my guy, just not the one you expected. And I choose him over the company. I choose *him*."

This weight that had been sitting on my shoulders for I didn't know how long, lifted the moment I said it. If I had a mike, I would have dropped it. I wasn't sure what I'd do after working for Sun Valley my whole life, but I needed to go find Clay more than I needed to figure that out right now.

I ran out and jumped in my truck. The beauty started right up, and I peeled out of the parking lot, waiting impatiently for the slow gate out of the property to open up for me. Clay didn't answer his phone, but that didn't worry me until I reached his house and he wasn't there. I even did the whole jumping on my tip-toes and checking through the garage door windows to see if his truck was inside the garage. It wasn't.

He didn't answer the door, and he still wasn't answering his phone. I sank down onto his front lawn and put my shaky hands together. I'd told my dad and Parker they were a bunch of hotheads, and I'd chewed them out, and then left, because that's what I did best. I was the biggest hothead of them all. Maybe I should start thinking about all the stupid decisions that led me here.

I didn't regret speaking up for Clay about ownership, but I certainly hadn't respected him in the way I went about it. And my constant warring with Parker was the reason the meeting today had gone downhill so fast. I had tattled on Parker's latest purchase, and he had tattled on my relationship with Clay. It was a continuation of the same battle that had always led us nowhere, and we'd just let it ruin the one person who cared about us the most.

Clay had always been the glue in the middle, holding us all together, but that wasn't a position anyone could hold forever. Or should hold.

Pulling out a clump of grass, I continued to worry. I needed to tell Clay all this, and patience had never been a strong suit of mine. It killed me, knowing Clay was out there having just lost his job, his best friend, and his plans for the future. Did he think he was losing me, too?

I couldn't tell him how much he meant to me if I couldn't find him.

CHAPTER 29

CLAY

Knowing I'd be sought out at my house, I'd driven aimlessly for a while, but I finally stopped at my grandparents' house and idled at the curb. I hadn't given them any notice of my coming. I had no idea what I'd even say if they asked. But I stayed put, and it didn't take long before my grandmother came outside and gave me an impatient wave. Loiterers must be dealt with, after all, even related ones. I rolled down my passenger window and attempted to smile.

"Are you coming in?" she asked.

I shrugged.

Instead of berating me for my lack of decision-making skills, she tilted her head and took me in like the pathetic specimen I was. "Clayton, come inside. You're wasting gas."

That was true. And if I was jobless, I didn't have gas money to burn. I turned off my truck and followed her into the house, taking a moment to study my mom's picture in its frame like I always did before sitting on the uncomfortable couch. What was I doing here?

"Come talk to Clay," I heard Grandma murmur to Grandpa in the kitchen. "I've never seen him sad. Stoic, yes, but not sad."

"What should I say?" Grandpa asked, clearly at a loss.

Despite the progress we'd made, it didn't change the reality of who they were. My grandparents didn't deal with feelings. Those were things you waited out. Maybe that's why I'd never let them see me sad, or mad, or even ecstatically happy before.

Was I sad now? I supposed I was. For one week, I'd forgotten all the reasons why dating Lauren would be a bad idea. But today had been illusion-wrecking day. I couldn't have it all. Maybe I couldn't have any of it. After all, wasn't I sitting here hiding from Lauren? I pulled out my phone and stared at it. I still wasn't ready to talk to anyone with the last name Harwood. Not yet.

"Clay, I have some things I'm getting rid of. Can you take them to the donation center for me?" Grandma asked, coming in with a box.

I quickly took it from her hands. "Of course. I'll go right now."

"Not yet. Sit some more. I have a few odds and ends to go through. Can you wait?" She blinked up at me, and it was the concern I saw there that did me in. She didn't just want me to wait for more junk, she wanted me to wait here until I felt better. I put the box on the floor and sat back down, running my hands through my hair until it stood on end. I could not cry. Not in front of her.

Grandpa chose that moment to shuffle in, and he sat down next to me. "You have any truck pictures to show me, Clayton?"

I swallowed before speaking. "No. Actually, I… quit today."

Grandma gave a small gasp. "But you've always worked there."

"Maybe it's time I do something else."

"That depends on why you quit," Grandpa said in his gravelly, always reasonable voice. "Quitting can be a positive or a negative thing. So can staying."

They were quiet, waiting for my answer. The ticking of the clock and the leering of the Nutcracker doll didn't help. The truth finally stumbled out of me because silence was worse.

"John Harwood found out I was dating Lauren. He didn't like that because… well, because he had invited me, Lauren, and Parker to be owners in the company. Originally, it was just going to be Lauren and Parker, but he invited me into the club today. And then promptly kicked me back out of it."

"The club?" Grandma frowned. "What club?"

"I think he's being sarcastic." Grandpa turned to look at me. "You thought you were kin, but you're not. Is that why you quit today?"

I nodded, not liking it spelled out in all its embarrassment.

Grandma clucked her tongue. "Your mother was an only child, too. She used to play with a family of eight kids across the street. There was nothing she loved more than to blend in with the bunch of them. Half the time, the parents didn't know she was there until I called to have them send her home."

Another tether to her, besides the color of our eyes and our strong chins. I wondered why my grandparents never had any other kids, but it wasn't the sort of thing you could ask.

Grandpa cleared his throat. "Is John mad because you kept it a secret, or is he mad because he doesn't want you dating his daughter?"

"I don't know."

"You didn't ask?"

"No." I didn't stay long enough to. Grandpa's question made me realize how impulsive I'd been. I'd left Lauren there to deal with our mess. I'd pursued her, secretly, and then when it all came out today, I ditched and ran. I had turned off my phone, didn't go to my house, didn't call. I even thought maybe she'd assumed the worst about me like the rest of her family. Some boyfriend I was.

"I need to go." I jumped to my feet and picked up Grandma's box. "Thanks for listening."

They nodded, looking confused by my sudden shift in mood.

Grandpa clapped me lightly on the shoulder. "Olsen men do better when they're employed, son. 'Bout drove your grandma nuts back in ninety-three when the postal service let me go.

Finding work again saved our marriage."

I nodded to reassure him I understood. "Point taken. I will definitely be working somewhere the next time you see me."

"Good. Good."

Grandma darted over to the mantel. "One more thing for the box, Clayton. I don't want this anymore."

She came back with the Nutcracker doll and placed it in the box I was holding. The thing stared up at me with his freaky white teeth and snowy eyebrows. Really? After all this time of being chronically creeped out by the thing, he was going away, just like that?

"You can keep him if you'd like. I know you've spent a lot of time looking at it. That's why I kept him for so long."

I shook my head, not believing what I was hearing. "No, I don't want to keep him. Thanks though. I'll make sure he gets donated." *Into the ground somewhere far, far away.*

All these years I'd spent locked in a losing staring contest with a doll, when I could have just said something to Grandma and ended it. What else wasn't I speaking up about?

CHAPTER 30

LAUREN

My worry was starting to turn into irritation. I could go home to my apartment and wait for Clay to come or call, but what if he came here after I drove off? He'd quit. I'd quit. He'd stormed off. I'd stormed off. And yet I felt out of sync with him and ticked off that he was shutting me out.

When the stubborn came out in me, it was hard to turn off. I decided to wait him out, even if I was here all night. But after ten minutes of sitting with nothing to do, I started worrying about all the work that wasn't getting done at the job I'd just quit. I logged into the system while I still could and went through the equipment intakes, making sure everything was accounted for, and that the equipment slated for rental the next day was ready. It was easier to focus on things like that than think about resumes and job searches. Was that going to be my reality tomorrow?

The rumble of Clay's truck coming down the road almost caught me off guard. I closed up my computer, dropped it on the passenger seat of my truck, slammed the door shut, and ran for the hibiscus bushes on the left side of Clay's porch. There was just enough room to duck behind the tallest one. The element of surprise was going to be a lot less surprising with my truck parked in his driveway, but I couldn't help myself. Somehow, just sitting on his porch glaring up at him would not be nearly as satisfying.

He pulled into the spot next to my truck and got out, shutting his door behind him. Although I couldn't quite see him yet, I could hear the scuff of his boots approaching.

"Lauren?" he called out.

Just a little closer, buddy.

I had enough common sense to let him see it was me in the half-second before I took a flying leap and tackled him into the flowerbed on the opposite side of the porch. It's not like I had a death wish. I just wanted revenge.

We both went down, and Clay groaned. "Thanks for killing the landscaping. And my back."

"Thanks for not answering your phone."

"I wasn't ready." He reached up and tucked a strand of hair behind my ear, but it just fell back out again with me leaning over him.

"And now you are, Mr. High-and-Mighty?"

He rolled me over and stared down into my eyes. I was getting dirt in my hair, but that thought was lost as he dipped his head and kissed me with the certainty of someone who had just given up everything to be with me.

The relief that brought made me realize some of my frustration had been fear. What if he'd decided this was too hard and I wasn't worth it?

"You don't hate me?" I whispered. "I screwed up everything."

Clay smiled down at me. "No, you didn't. I should have realized Parker would figure it out. His detective skills are top-notch when it comes to getting you in trouble."

"I'm sorry about what he said, and that my dad let him say it. I chewed them out after you left."

"I shouldn't have taken off like that and left you there to deal with it."

"I quit, too."

Clay's eyes widened at that revelation. "You can't do that. You're an owner."

"Not yet. And I'm not going to spend the rest of my life working with them if it means losing you. I'm done fighting with them, and I'm done with secrets."

Clay sat up and helped me up with him. "So, we're both unemployed? That's a bummer."

I laughed. "I told you dating me was a bad idea."

"Oh yeah? When? Because I recall you saying there were no outs. That we were doing this no matter what."

"Yeah, but I'm not holding you to 'no matter what' unless I do a better job at this girlfriend thing."

Clay raised an eyebrow. "You're looking to improve?"

"You told me not to butt in on your behalf, and I did it anyway. I was so afraid you wouldn't ask for something that was rightfully yours. I'm sorry I'm a Harwood and we just do things, and then when everything blows up, we get into a wrestling match next to the explosion."

Clay pulled me into him and hugged me. "Don't be sorry for being you. But speaking of asking for things…" He jumped to his feet. "Hang on a second, I have something to show you." He jogged over to his truck and opened up the passenger side door before returning to where I was sitting with something behind his back. "I got this from my grandparents' house. That's where I went instead of coming here."

I tried to get a look at whatever it was, but he easily blocked me. Even knowing he was enjoying my curiosity didn't stop me from hopping to my feet and starting up a pointless game of keep-away. After a minute, I gave up and turned my back on him. Big mistake.

"Hello, Lauren," Clay sing-songed in a high-pitched voice. He tapped my shoulder with whatever it was, and suddenly the leering face of a Nutcracker doll was in my face, making me scream a little, and Clay laugh a lot.

"Please tell me you're not taking up ventriloquism to express your inner feelings. Why do you have that?" I grabbed for it, but Clay held it out of reach.

"My grandmother put it in a box for charity and asked me to drop it off for her. All these years of not telling her how much I hated the thing, and she tosses it aside on her own."

"I'm not sure I'm following. Are you wanting me to help you punt it across the yard? Because I would love to help with that."

"Later. Right now, I'm going to face one of my fears and just tell you. I love you, Lauren. And it's okay if you can't say it back. I'm done being afraid of going for what I want."

Clay tended to gesture when he talked, and the Nutcracker doll waving in his hands made it really hard to take him seriously. It also made him impossible not to love in that moment. "I love you, too. Way to make this awesome moment weird with your creepy doll." I stole it out of his hands and copied his motions until he tackled me into the grass.

When Parker and Dad pulled up to the curb in their apology caravan two minutes later, Clay was still chasing me around the yard with the Nutcracker doll. What a day.

CHAPTER 31

CLAY

The entire Harwood clan had never been to my house all at once, but that's what happened. Charlotte arrived in her sedan a few seconds after John and Parker and immediately threw her arms around me and Lauren in a group hug on my lawn.

"I saw this coming, but you're still both busted for not telling me," she whispered.

"Sorry," Lauren whispered back.

Behind us, John was shuffling from one foot to the other. It was only a theory, but I was pretty sure he had called Charlotte hoping for some sympathy, and got an earful and instructions to get everyone over here instead. There were few reasons John ever left work, and I had to imagine Charlotte was one of them.

John cleared his throat. "Connor and Melissa are on their way here. Clay, do you mind if we all come inside and talk with you?"

Melissa and Connor were coming, too? Lauren's fingers, which were laced with mine, gave a little squeeze.

"Yeah, sure. Come in." I led the way, grabbing my laptop and socks off the couch before motioning for them to sit.

Lauren and I sat across from the three of them on the love

seat, and thus began a really, really awkward pause where no one wanted to look at each other, except for Charlotte, who had nothing to be ashamed of.

Parker looked like he was ready to jump ship. I knew him. He wanted to apologize, but not with an audience, and not with *this* audience. So, I did him a favor. While John and Charlotte started up small talk about how nice my house was, you know, for a bachelor who'd bought a tiny fixer-upper, I texted Parker.

Clay: I'm sorry I didn't tell you about Lauren.

Parker pulled out his phone and frowned at my message before typing out a response.

Parker: I'm sorry I told John. That was low. And also assuming you had some sinister motive for dating her.

Clay: No motives. I promise. As it is, I've been holding back for years.

Parker's head came up, and he gave me a look of pure long-suffering.

Parker: No explanation needed. Or wanted. Ever.

Clay: Fair enough.

Lauren caught on to our conversation, and pulled out her own phone. A few seconds later, she'd put us in a group thread.

Lauren: You two made nice yet?

Parker: None of your business. Stay out of this, bossy pants.

Clay: Hey now. Only I get to call her that.

Lauren: <laugh emoji>

Parker: <Puke emoji>

John studied the three of us and our phones. "Are you texting each other? You're all right here in the same room."

Parker rolled his eyes. "Go ahead and insert your millennial joke."

John sighed and said nothing, looking out of his element. Every few seconds, his eyes flitted to Lauren's hand on my knee, and once again, I wondered how much of a disappointment I was compared to the mythical perfect man he'd picked out for her, one who wasn't supposed to show up for another five years or so.

But I didn't fear the future anymore. We'd figure it out, one awkward conversation at a time.

Connor and Melissa, with Jax and Raelyn in tow, finally came through the door, taking the kitchen table chairs and dragging them over to us in the living room. They had fast-food bags, and a diaper bag, and basically looked like they were on hour fourteen of a long car trip, instead of a short jaunt across town. Jax, a little sweaty and sleepy, was placed in my arms. I patted his back and smiled at him, getting a goofy smile in return. This. This little guy and the spitfire sitting next to me made me feel like everything was going to be okay.

Connor glanced around. "Is anyone working today? My extended lunch break has to end at some point, so let's make this quick. No offense, Clay. You two have my blessing. I've been telling Melissa for years it was gonna happen."

Melissa looked rightly annoyed. "No, you said it had already happened, and they've been secretly on and off for years. And *I* said if that was the case I'd be able to tell."

All eyes turned to us to settle the debate.

"Nope, this is new," Lauren said, holding up our joined hands.

Melissa clapped. "That's right. Mama's getting a full body massage tonight."

Connor groaned right along with the rest of us, but the look of fake outrage he gave Melissa fooled exactly no one. Sometimes they were worse than John and Charlotte with their flirting.

Parker, who'd clearly had all the secondary romance he could stand, chucked the couch pillow he'd been hugging at

Connor, and several things happened at once. Parker's bad aim meant Raelyn got a pillow to the face and dropped her soda—her orange soda that exploded all over her dress, her chair, Melissa next to her, and my carpet. And then there was the screaming. Lots of screaming.

CHAPTER 32

LAUREN

We weren't a big family, but boy, were we loud and intense sometimes, with all the subtlety of a social justice warrior in a Reddit forum. I wasn't sure what their plan was in coming here, but I doubted it was to destroy Clay's carpet. Orange soda did not forgive. The color wasn't coming out of Raelyn's arms and face, let alone anything fabric. She looked like an angry carrot. An angry, screaming carrot. Like one of those mandrakes they uproot in Harry Potter that made students faint from the noise.

Her crying made Jax cry, and Connor took him from Clay while Melissa and Raelyn headed off to make a new mess in Clay's guest bathroom. The rest of us continued either mopping up the carpet or criticizing the technique everyone else was using. For the record, I was swabbing, and Parker was criticizing. Shocker.

Clay's hand snaked around my waist and expertly extracted me from the situation. It was highly attractive how sneaky he could be. I don't think anyone noticed him do it, except for Parker, who wisely chose not to look.

Clay led me behind the couch and pulled me down to sit next to him before cupping my face with his hands. "Your family is insane."

I laughed. "Was that news to you?"

"No." He leaned in to kiss me. I'm sure he meant to just give me a peck, but I didn't allow him to stop there, and he didn't exactly mind the redirection.

"Where are Clay and Lauren?" John suddenly asked, loud and paranoid. It was the voice of a parent noticing a missing Sharpie and a toddler not in the room.

Kissing isn't exactly a silent activity, and I extracted my arms and lips from Clay just in time to look up and see several faces staring down at us from over the couch. Busted.

Ignoring my flushed face, I pointed up at all of them. "It's his carpet you ruined. Would you rather have him yelling at you to scrub harder? And why is everyone at his house anyway?"

Clay got to his feet and then helped me up. "They're here for a company meeting." He looked at my dad, and some sort of understanding passed between them.

I shook my head. "No, they're here for a family meeting. Isn't that why we waited for Connor and Melissa?"

"It's both," my dad confirmed.

This made Clay deflate a little, and I think I understood why. Those two things would always be intertwined, and he only fit into one of those categories. With some alarm, I realized the questions my dad would probably throw at us in a minute. Were we getting married? What would happen if we broke up? Could we all stay friends if that happened, or would Clay drift out of our lives, and it would be all my fault?

It wasn't fair. Those were questions for the two of us to figure out together, with time, and trust, and without my family poking at us like lab rats. I wanted to date Clay, not file daily reports on him. I could see today's update now.

Relationship status update #1. *Clay told me he loved me today. I replied in the affirmative. Annoying family interrupts the happy occasion with messes and impertinent questions.*

I'd already told them I was choosing Clay. And that meant choosing the best chance at our happiness. I needed to be serious about quitting. I couldn't go back. I wouldn't.

When Melissa and Raelyn came in wearing Clay's old basketball T-shirts and everyone sat back down, Dad immediately started in. "Clay and Lauren, I don't accept your resignations. I still want you both as owners. But I do have some concerns."

"Don't say them." I shook my head. "I don't want to hear them. And if I don't work for you, they're none of your business."

"But—"

"Nope."

My dad's face began to turn red. Especially when Clay started in.

"I'm not coming back either."

I clutched his arm. "You should. Anyone can do my job, but they need you."

"Untrue. Your job is important, too."

There was a long silence. Nobody was winning in this situation. Maybe by quitting we had made things worse, but I couldn't see a way around it. Even Connor and Melissa looked concerned.

Parker cleared his throat. "You might not need us, but I need you. Both of you." He leaned forward, looking like he was about to puke. "Just come back."

Parker wasn't one to show he needed anybody. Ever. How could I say no to that? Tears stung in my eyes, but I refused to let them fall. Parker would never forgive me if I let everyone see what his words meant to me.

Clay looked at me before turning back to my dad. "I want a year."

That was met with lots of blank faces, including mine.

"I want a year where the three of us are apprentice owners. No paperwork signed. No discussions of relationships. We start making company decisions together and see if we can work as a team. And after a year, we'll have this conversation again."

"But what if I die before then?" Dad looked legitimately concerned about it, and if I didn't know him so well, I'd fear he had some secret fatal illness. But he didn't need that to worry. He worried about everything. It was almost like he'd been abducted years ago by financial planner aliens and had permanent fear implanted in his head.

Clay gestured to my mom. "Then you leave the company to Charlotte, and let her sort it out. But don't die."

Dad nodded, looking repentant and proud, all at the same time. "You're a good one, Clay."

"Took you long enough to realize it, Dad." I leaned into Clay.

We Harwoods could only take so much mushy, so it was no surprise when Connor stood, bouncing Jax in his arms. "Sounds like we have a plan. Sorry about the carpet." Connor murmured something to Melissa, and they began gathering up all their assorted mess.

"We'll get these shirts back to you, Clay." Melissa tiptoed over and kissed my forehead. "I want all the dirty details, girl. Call me later."

Oh, I would. She'd hear about Noble, too, and his obnoxious flowers.

Once they left, the conversation immediately went back to shop talk, and when Clay and I planned to get back into work today. I'd been unemployed for an hour, and my dad made it sound like I was wasting my life away.

After a few minutes, I somewhat lovingly shooed Dad, Mom, and Parker towards the door. "Dad, you told Noble I was available for a lunch date today, so don't give me this crap about missing work. We'll be back when we're back."

I shut the door on them and turned around to face Clay.

His eyebrow raised. "Noble asked you out?"

"Yeah. I turned him down. He didn't take it well."

"And I missed it?"

"A year, huh?" I said, changing the subject. Ain't nobody had time for Noble Tuttle—not for a lunch date, and not in this conversation, when we had more important things to discuss.

Clay shrugged, looking sort of self-conscious. "I didn't exactly run that plan by you, did I?"

"I'm not mad, I'm just curious why a year. Where do you see us in a year?"

"Hopefully ready for ownership."

"Well, yeah. But where do you see the two of us in a year?" I inched closer to Clay, which added to his nervousness about where I was going with this.

"The two of us?" Clay's voice cracked a little, making me want to dig harder.

"Yeah, the two of us."

"I see us happy. Don't you?"

I smiled. "I do."

"Good." Clay kissed me, thinking the conversation was over.

I waited until he moved to the kitchen to look for something for us to eat. This was our lunch date, after all.

"Clay, do you see us married in a year?"

"What?" He whirled around and studied me carefully, likely waiting for the punchline. The fact that it was hope he was trying to conceal from me, and not panic, did something to my insides. He wanted to marry me. He did. His eyes said someday, like he'd been picturing it all along, and was only waiting until I could see it, too.

He approached me and poked me lightly in the side. "Don't make jokes about the M word, Laur."

"I'm not." And I wasn't. I bit my lip. I'd have to be careful with my wording. He'd offered me his heart only recently, and I intended to take good care of it for a long time. But that also meant being honest about the state of mine. "I'm not saying I'm ready. I'm just saying, it's not... off the table."

It was Clay's turn to look mischievous. He'd sensed my nervousness, and he stared into my eyes, daring me to admit it. He could stare all day for all I cared. I'd admit nothing.

"Maybe we need an in-between term." Clay got down on one knee, and he wouldn't get up no matter how much I tugged on him. "What? Am I making you nervous?"

"Nope. I'm fine."

Laughing, he asked, "What would a British person say when they're not ready to be engaged but not opposed to the idea?"

"They'd say get off this kitchen floor right now before I start planning revenge. That Nutcracker doll, he's going in your sheets. One day, you'll wake up and find him next to you. Staring. Forever."

Clay tugged me down into his arms and kissed me. "Lauren," he whispered. "Once again, just a bit of advice." He was laughing so hard he could barely finish. "If you're planning a surprise attack on someone, it's best to actually keep it a surprise."

I slapped his shoulder, which did no good. He just kept on laughing.

"Hey, I jumped you from the bushes, dude. Today. Bet you didn't see that coming."

"Playing the long game, are we?"

I kissed the underside of his neck where a bit of scruff was starting to appear. "Always, Olsen. Always."

EPILOGUE — ALMOST ONE YEAR LATER

JENNY

"You two are the least sneaky PDAers I have ever seen. Just make out already and be quiet about it." I smiled to myself and went back to watching the traffic in front of me, studiously avoiding my rearview mirror.

I should have known something was up when Clay decided the front passenger seat was the perfect spot for the breakables. *Oh, and you drive, Jen. We'll hold onto the house plants back here.* More like hide behind them. Clay and Lauren had been exchanging longing looks, kissing each other's fingers, and whispering secret nothings to each other the whole drive. Disgusting. Adorably disgusting. They'd be unbearable as newlyweds.

"Sorry, Jen." Lauren leaned forward and squeezed my shoulder. "Have you picked a new roommate?"

"Not yet." We'd met with four girls today between moving tasks, and I couldn't decide who should replace Lauren as my roommate. If it was up to me, I'd stick Lauren in a 3D printer and make a clone. Part of it was how much I loved her, but part of it was how much I hated change. I didn't want to work out the sticky details of how to live with someone else. Did we share food? Would we wait up for each other like Lauren and I did? Who got the remote? Could we fart in front of each other? Could I use the word fart? I'd once had a summer camp bunkmate who made everyone say 'toot' the entire three weeks we were together.

"Jen, you look like you're trying to split the atom with your mind up there."

"Just preparing to merge, Clay. I'm fine."

"You sure?" Lauren added. "Air your grievances. You have my permission."

I definitely didn't want to do that. Everything that was making Lauren over-the-top happy was making me sad. And none of that was her fault or required her to change anything. She was a week away from her wedding and giddy about moving her stuff into Clay's house. Well, *their* house now. This Friday was the last night Lauren and I would share an apartment. Instead of a bachelorette party, we'd planned an epic sleepover. Melissa and Raelyn, Charlotte, and a few of Lauren's closest friends would camp out on the floor with us. I would be super fun and happy the whole time, even if it killed me.

But maybe I could tease her about the Valentine's thing.

"I want to know why you two picked Valentine's Day to get married. I'm going to be alone, on the day of love, at a wedding. And no, I'm not drumming up a plus one at the last minute so don't ask."

"Parker is—"

"Nope." Ew. "He's like a brother to me. And not in the way you looked at Clay." I laughed at Lauren's grouchy face. There had been no hiding it. That first day I saw them together, when Clay came to give her a ride to work, it was like the puzzle that was Lauren's dating life found its missing piece. He was it for her. She just hadn't admitted it to herself yet. For her, every other guy was gray and fuzzy, and Clay was in vibrant color.

"I don't even like Valentine's," Lauren said, leaning her head on Clay's shoulder. "It just happened to be the only Saturday this month that we don't have work or family stuff. Plus the deal we got on our honeymoon trip sort of made it perfect. Do you hate me?"

"Of course not. I was teasing. Weddings are fun." The Valentines thing hadn't even bothered me until recently. Up until two weeks ago, I'd had a boyfriend. Or, at least someone I'd dated long enough to start calling him that in my head. He broke up with me over text, no reason given, though I could think of a few. We had been lukewarm at best. Pleasant together. Consistent.

Love was this scary and beautiful thing that existed all around me. I could see it. I could read about it. But I'd never experienced it before. The closest I'd come was—"Noah!" I swerved a little when my eyes registered who was driving in the lane next to me. I would know that forest green Toyota minivan anywhere. I'd made fun of it on a weekly basis, after all. Along with its driver.

Clay and Lauren sat up straight and held onto their plants, looking concerned.

"I'm fine. I'm fine." I was so not fine. Noah had left six months ago. He'd taken a promotion in California and ditched me like the coward he was. Since he'd left, I'd been stuck in carpool awkwardness with Sadie and Dan. Noah had been the jelly in the sandwich of our group. Without him, things were a little dry and tasteless. I'd missed him, and I hated that I'd missed him.

Thanks to my driving flub, Noah had spotted me too. I glanced over and caught his hesitant smile. It should be hesitant. We'd had a MOMENT. And then... nothing. I hadn't made the next move, and he hadn't made the next move, and then he left.

I sped up until he was in my rearview.

"Was that... Noah. Like, Noah?" Lauren asked.

195

"Nope. That was nobody."

Except now my phone was ringing, and even though I'd removed Noah as a contact, I recognized his number calling.

Thank you, lovely readers. Reviews are much appreciated. If you enjoyed Clay and Lauren's story, don't miss going back in time and finding out how Connor and Melissa met in Worst Neighbor Ever. All my author links are here: https://linktr.ee/rjohn

Other titles by Rachel John:

Engaging Mr. Darcy
Emma the Matchmaker
Persuading the Captain
Dashing into Disaster

An Unlikely Alliance
Her Charming Distraction
Protector of Her Heart
Pretending He's Mine

Matchmaker for Hire
Bethany's New Reality
Gorgeous and the Geek

The Stand-in Christmas Date
The Christmas Bachelor Auction
The Christmas Wedding Planners
The Accidental Christmas Match Up

ABOUT THE AUTHOR

Rachel John lives in Arizona with her husband and four kids. Besides hanging out with the characters in her head, she likes to jam out to music that annoys her kids, read romance books, occasionally go running as part of her zombie apocalypse prepping, and work on family history. She has a fairly useless English Literature degree from Arizona State University but learned the most about writing and craft from the awesome writer community online. Rachel is most active on Instagram with the handle @racheljohnwrites. Come say hi!

THANK YOU

A special thank you to my developmental editor, Jacque Stevens at www.sjacquebooks.com and to my proofreader, Jessica Martinez (facebook.com/everywordinitsplace). I've also been overwhelmed by the support from so many Bookstagrammers on Instagram who have been my cheerleaders on this project. It's a scary thing to trust people with characters who have been living in your head just for you. Thank you readers! I love what I do.

Printed in Great Britain
by Amazon